HEART OF SILVER

KIERNAN KELLY

EVIL PLOT BUNNY

HEART OF SILVER

An imprint of Evil Plot Bunny

PO Box 722

Loughman, FL 33837

Copyright 2020 by Kiernan Kelly

Cover by Designs EE

Published with permission

ISBN: 978-1-951777-23-4

First Printing: June 2020

Printed in the USA

❀ Created with Vellum

PROLOGUE

Wind blew as if the mountain were exhaling a long, cold breath. It rustled the foliage of the cove forest, and as a result, a shower of brilliantly colored leaves of sugar maple, beech, oak, and more fluttered down to cover the ground in a vibrant, multihued carpet. They crunched under Mac's feet with the age-old music of late autumn.

The mountain was beautiful this time of year, but the leaves were a reminder that winter wasn't long off. All too soon that cold wind would turn bitter enough to steal the breath from your lungs and burn your skin like fire. Already the blue skies overhead darkened with clouds belly-heavy with the season's first snow. Mac could smell the coming storm on the wind, too, and there was no telling how bad it would be. If a blizzard swept across the mountain, it could bury everything in a smooth, thick blanket of white. The last thing Mac needed was to get caught out in the elements unprepared.

The people of the Jewel Creek pack called winter the "season of death," and appropriately so. Not everyone survived the bitterly cold season. More than one wolf he knew had succumbed to the harsh weather and empty stom-achs winter usually brought with it. Some caught out in howling blizzards never made it home again.

A shudder rippled through him, and he shook himself, trying to cast off a sudden feeling of foreboding as well as the chill. Not even his wolf-self's thick coat could protect him from the rapidly dropping temperature or the sense of coming trouble in his gut. He could do nothing but keep on, so he ducked his head into the wind and continued padding across the forested hillside, making his way toward a tiny, sheltered valley he knew lay nearby.

Eons ago, a sparkling stream cut a meandering path across the mountain, and winter snows and spring thaws eventually carved out the valley the Jewel Creek pack claimed as their territory. It was small and densely forested, and because of the conveniently close supply of fresh water and abundant wildlife, the elders of the Jewel Creek pack were attracted to the remote area in the West Virginia moun-tains sometime in the late 1600s. Back then, the forest had been thick with white-tailed deer, black bear, wild boar, fox, raccoon, moles, bats, turkeys, several species of squirrel, and much more. Even the occasional elk or moose could be found wandering through the stands of black cherry, ash, and hickory. The Jewel Creek pack settled easily into the land of plenty, chasing away the competing timber and red wolves and naming their new home Wolf Valley. They could have -- maybe *should* have -- named it after their pack and call it Jewel Valley, but the settlers had a streak of nostalgia about them. For time immemorial, no matter where they lived, their land was called Wolf Something-or-other -- Wolf Mountain, Wolf Bay, Wolf Bog, and so forth. They chose to continue the tradition in this New World.

They cleared an area near a bend in the stream and built their homes. The valley provided everything they needed—

privacy, timber, food, and space to roam when the moon called to their wolf-selves.

Game slowly grew sparser over time. Humans were the cause, for the most part. They spread like the fire-pox, settling in hollers all over Appalachia until not even secluded Wolf Valley was safe from their destructive ways. Humans hunted the forest for pelts, stealing food from mouths of the Jewel Creek pack in the process. They cut timber and over-fished the streams. They set out jagged-toothed metal traps sometimes, catching unwary pack members instead of animals as Jeb Prower, a grizzled wolf in his forties, found out the hard way. After he got caught in one, he had to chew his own foot off to escape. The pack leaders made Jeb an omega after that and forced him to forage for roots and fruit or gather firewood with the pups instead of hunting. Although Jeb's three remaining paws were strong, pack tradition—which had the force of law—relegated deformed or disfigured wolves to omega status. It was the way of nature—the weakest wolves were always forced to the outer fringes of the pack. It had been a long way to fall for Jeb, who'd been born into an alpha family. He never recovered from it.

Worse, as everyone in the pack knew, once an omega, always an omega. There was no way back for him. Pack law wouldn't allow it. Mac never understood the rule. What made alphas better than deltas, or gammas better than omegas? What made them different? Nothing Mac could see, for sure. It seemed arbitrary and crazy to him. Even physically weak members could recover or, if not, contribute in other, equally important ways.

Jeb killed himself the next winter, walking out of his cabin and into the forest in the middle of a ferocious snow-storm wearing nothing but his man-skin. He hadn't made it very far out of the settlement before freezing to death. Pack hunters found him after the following spring thaw, frozen solid and skin burned black by the cold.

Mac sneezed and shook his head. He understood how Jeb felt, at least partially. He knew what it was like to be an omega wolf. Being born to Angus and Sylva, members of the Fuller clan, had seen to it. They were the lowest-ranked omega family in the pack. Everyone thought they were trash, and truth be told, some of them were, but not all. Not him. Not his ma or pa. His pa brewed 'shine up on the north side of the mountain, but at least that took some skill and earned a few much-needed dollars for the family when Pa took the jugs down the mountain to the human village to sell.

However, even Mac admitted his brothers, Rafe and Peregrine, were lazy good-for-nothings. They were perfectly happy doing nothing and begging for scraps when their empty bellies grumbled. They drank too much of Pa's liquor and weren't above making occasional raids on human villages with Mac's cousins, either, stealing whatever they could find. They fought a lot, too, picking fights with any omega they thought they could easily take either by size or surprise. They were sneaky, lowdown, cheating bastards, and Mac despised them for the grief they'd caused him and his family.

Then again, lots of pack members seemed born to violence. Fights were always breaking out, mostly over stupid things, too, at least in Mac's opinion. It seemed to him as if pack members sometimes had a cup of crazy for breakfast.

Not Mac. He prided himself on being neither crazy nor stupid, not a beggar or a thief, and in his mind, he was just as good as anybody else in the pack. So were his mother, father, and baby sister, Tabby. Not that he didn't fight when he had to—he did and usually won. Unlike Jeb, he refused to bend under the weight of the omega stigma. Maybe it'd been harder for Jeb, since Jeb hadn't been born an omega. Growing up, if anyone bullied him, he fought back. God knew he had the scars to prove it too.

He was only sixteen, but he'd already been in more scuffles than he could count. Pa said he needed to accept things the way they were, the way they'd always been, and Ma agreed, but Mac couldn't understand it and couldn't force himself to believe it. Again and again, the same question rose up—what made some of the pack members better than others? They all bled red, right? At least, he knew *he* did— bright red and, at least in his case, often.

Mac paused and whined. He lifted his right front paw and licked a bite mark just over his wrist. Damn it, it was a deep one. It was still bleeding a little, even though the fight had been over for more than an hour. Luc Alden put it there, a souvenir of Mac's latest skirmish. He stuck it in a snowbank for a moment, hoping the cold would stem the flow of blood.

Pa was going to stripe his hide when word got out he'd been fighting alphas again. Not that Mac had a choice in the matter. What did Pa expect him to do? Just roll over and show his belly? Take their insults and smile? Not fucking likely.

Besides, he didn't start it. Luc and his buddies, JJ Alden, Will Butten, Blue Standish, and a few others, had cornered Mac out by Jewel Creek's far bend and taunted him, calling him a dog among other things and ordering him to fetch a stick they threw. When he refused, they tried to take his camera. His camera! They might as well have tried to take his right arm.

He glanced at the old beat-up Nikon he held. He'd found it in a trash can down in the city. For six months, he'd diligently scanned sidewalks for fallen change and picked up bottles to sell for recycling until he'd saved enough to bring the camera into a shop and get it fixed. It was his most treasured possession, and he would bite the arm off anyone who tried to take it from him.

His family thought he was crazy to fight over a piece of junk like the Nikon, but he thought it was nuts not to. A guy had to have something to call his own, right? Something to feel pride over, especially when there was so little else in his life of any worth.

Besides, there were crazier people than Mac in the pack. Just last week, Mabel Adams had up and decided her henhouse was haunted and burned that damned thing to the ground, eggs, chickens, and all. And last spring hadn't Pete McElroy picked up his shotgun and put a hole clean through his bathroom wall because he was convinced the man looking back at him from the mirror over the sink was an imposter?

Yeah, there was lots of foolishness in the pack. Mac figured he was in good company. Not for the first time, he wondered whether people were the same all over or if was only the Jewel Creek pack who seemed dogpaddling in a pool of insanity.

He moved on, trying to ignore the taste of his own blood in his mouth. He needed to get home before the storm broke. A thicket of thorny scrub tore at his fur, but he pushed past it and finally emerged from the wood into a clearing.

Wolf Valley lay before him, nestled between two densely forested mountains like a babe cuddled in its mother's arms. Wood cabins were built in concentric semicircles around a small clearing, with the largest cabins in the first semicircle, decreasing in size in each subsequent ring. The alphas, of course, claimed the largest cabins, followed by the gammas and deltas. The omegas lived in the tarpaper shanties making up the farthest semicircle from the clearing.

A sparkling stream the pack called Jewel Creek meandered to the right of the settlement and ran the entire length of the valley. Mac noticed the edges of the stream were already beginning to crust with ice. He figured by the coming storm's end, the creek would be fully iced over. Getting water would be more difficult. The snow around the settlement would soon become dirty from the day-to-day living of the residents and their animals. The omegas would have to cut a hole in the ice on the stream to draw up water for the pack to use for drinking, cooking, and washing. Sometimes, if they were lucky, someone might dangle a line into the hole and catch a fish. If they did, it would be salted and added to the pack's winter store of food.

He stopped for a moment and shifted to his human form. Shivering violently, his thin man-skin doing nothing to protect him from the frigid temperature, he retrieved the clothing he'd stashed inside a fallen, hollow tree trunk earlier. He dressed quickly, then continued into the village.

There was little movement among the cabins in the first three rows, apart from lazy blue curls of smoke rising from stovepipe chimneys and a few children playing here and there. The cold had already chased most people inside.

He skirted the quiet alpha, gamma, and delta sections of the settlement and walked to the final semicircle of buildings. Here among the omegas, life went on as usual, unaltered by the falling temperatures. Men split wood, tanned hides, and repaired tools while women churned butter and washed clothes, pushing the fabric with large paddles through vats of boiling water. During the warmer seasons, the clothes would be hung on lines outside to dry, but in the depths of winter when wet clothes could freeze solid outside, they were hung inside the omega shacks where the heat from the fireplace could dry them.

All except the very youngest omega children worked— their jobs were to scour the forest for dried deer and bear dung for fuel, collect armfuls of small branches for kindling, and help with whatever other chores or errands were needed. In the gardens beyond the last circle, a few women and children hunting for any half-frozen vegetables missed during the harvest.

Although he knew almost all of them would rather be warm inside, snuggled under quilts in front of the fireplace rather than working outside in the snow and cold, he also knew none of them had a choice. Work had to be done if the pack was to survive the winter, and the mantle of manual labor fell solely on the shoulders of the omegas.

The alphas did little besides hunt and oversee the rest of the pack. They upheld the rules of the pack, held court, and decided the fates of the other members. In effect, the alphas were the leaders, the monarchs. Their word was law and no one dared disobey.

The deltas smoked and dried the meat, put up the vegetables and fruits for winter, and prepared food for cooking. They used the cloth woven by the gammas to make clothing and quilts, sewing everything by hand.

The gammas cooked and served the food. They were extremely adept at weaving, taking the yarn spun by the omegas and weaving it at their large looms into sturdy fabric. They also dyed the fabric, using natural dyes from fruit, bark, and earth.

The omegas did virtually everything else. While the other members of the Jewel Creek pack sat in rockers placed comfortably close to fireplaces inside their homes, whittling or quilting, the omegas fought the cold to complete their backbreaking chores.

The unfairness of it weighed heavily on Mac. He hated being an omega, hated even more that he had no choice in the matter, had done nothing to deserve his status except be born, and could never do anything to better himself. The hopelessness of his life ate at him. He felt it burning away his soul like acid.

"There he is!"

He looked up at the sound of the voice. There was a small gathering of people standing outside the hovel he called home. His ma and pa were there, along with a couple of his aunts and uncles. Everyone except his mother was scowling at him. His ma looked frightened, and that worried him. More troubling still was the fact several alphas were present in the group—Gray Alden, the acknowledged leader of the Jewel Creek pack, and Alden's two right-hand men, John Winslow and Elias Minter. Enoch Standish was there, as well as Argyle, Blue's father, who stood nearby with an unmistakable expression of smugness on his face. Mac knew immediately word of his latest fight had reached the pack leaders already.

"Where have you been, Mac?" His father asked the question at the same time his mother whimpered, "Oh, Mac, what have you done?"

Alden stepped forward, his expression grim. Winslow and Minter stood just a pace behind him. "McKenna Fuller, you've done it this time. Gone and near bit my boy's ear off."

Mac grimaced and held up his arm. "I got bit too. It was a fight—"

"We know. You attacked Luc, unprovoked. He had every reason to defend himself. You're lucky he didn't tear your throat out." Alden's expression was both haughty and disdainful.

Mac understood at once and returned Alden's scowl with a sullen look of his own. It was a familiar scenario to him, one played out often over the years. No matter the truth of the situation, when an alpha and an omega got into a scuffle, it was always the omega's fault. The alpha was never to blame. How could they be? They were alphas, better than anyone else, superiority bred into their bones. They were the closest thing to royalty in the Jewel Creek pack and could do no wrong.

He didn't stand a chance. His skin crawled with anticipation of the whipping he was sure to get from his pa. That's what always happened before when he'd gotten into a fight. He waited nervously for his pa to order him to go cut a switch, but tried not to let his fear show. After a hard swallow, he lifted his chin and stared at Alden in defiance. If he was going to pay the price, he might as well let his side be heard, if not believed. "Luc came after *me*, not the other way 'round. Him and his friends, they cornered me, told me I had to fetch and tote like a good dog. I—"

Alden cut him off. "What you did was knock out one of Luc's incisors!"

There was a rumble of anger that seemed to feed Alden's fury. He became even more agitated, gesturing with short, angry jabs at Mac, and raised his voice, addressing the group of people at his back. "That's what happens when uppity omegas don't know their place. A fine, upstanding young man like Luc, full of promise and possibility, and now I'm going to have to take him down into the human city and get him a tooth implanted."

Mac almost smiled. "So, does that mean Luc is going to be demoted to an omega? I mean, alphas can't have fake teeth, can they?"

A hard fist swung out and clipped Mac on the jaw, dropping him where he stood. Alden stood over him, teeth bared. He looked about a half a heartbeat away from shifting. If he did, Mac was as good as dead. Nobody would dare try to stop a shifted pack leader mid-attack.

"You shut your mouth and listen to me, McKenna Fuller. The last thing this pack needs is another smart-mouth, good-for-nothing, loser omega running around, always causing trouble. Your brothers are bad enough, but at least they know their place. We don't want lowlifes like you starting fights with your betters and not contributing to the welfare of this community. You'll never be an asset to this pack, never earn your keep. You're useless. Worthless!" His lip curled over his teeth in a sneer. "You're banished. You hear me, boy? Get your ass out of the valley and off pack land, and don't you never come back. You do, and I'll kill you myself."

His mother cried out, and her sob turned into a howl as she shifted into her wolf-self, her clothing loosely draped and puddled over her wolf form. Hers was the only sympathetic cry Mac heard. The others in the small crowd growled and snarled at him, as if furious he still stood before them and wasn't scrambling away in fear like an omega should.

Mac's father squatted and threw his arms around Mac's mother to comfort her. He made no sound, but the grief and disappointment gleaming wetly in his eyes was almost too much for Mac to bear. Did his parents really believe what Alden was saying? That Mac was a worthless, troublemaking loser? That he was nothing but trash?

They must. Neither of them voiced any sort of dissent. No one stood up for him.

He backed away, first one step, then another. Tears burned at the corners of his eyes, and his chest tightened as anger pulsed within him. Well, fine. Good! Fuck them all. He didn't need them. He didn't need anybody.

Spinning on his heel, he dashed away, shifting midstep. He paused only long enough to fight his way out of his clothing and pick his camera up in his mouth. Then he ran, leaving nothing but the shredded remains of his clothing in his wake. For now, his grief was walled up behind a barricade of fury as he left the village and everything he'd ever known behind, but it would break free soon enough.

Snow fell in a thicker curtain just as he disappeared into

the forested mountainside. Deep in the wood, surrounded by nothing but silence, he howled his pain to the sky. He went on, having no choice but to leave or lay down on the cold, unforgiving ground and die.

Soon the snow became heavy, coating the ground with a smothering white blanket, and he knew it would obliterate any trace of his passing.

It would be as if he'd never been there at all.

CHAPTER 1

F *ifteen years later*
"Give me the hotness, baby. Smile like you can taste me. That's it."

The model's teeth flashed white and his vacuous expression deepening into the realm of deranged. His eyes narrowed, the veins in his neck bulging. His lips parted, and a thin line of drool snaked between them.

Mac sighed and lowered his camera. "Glen!"

His assistant scurried forward. "What's wrong?"

"He's fucking stoned again, That's what's wrong! How many times have I asked you to make sure the models are sober for shoots?" He waved his camera at Glen. "The only way I can use these shots is if we're shooting a spread for Narcotics Anonymous Magazine."

Glen blinked at him. "Today's shoot is for *Glamourize*, boss. I don't think NA has a magazine."

"Is *everyone* here high, including you? I was being sarcastic." Mac huffed and turned on his heel, thrusting his camera toward Glen's chest as he passed. "Call the agency and get someone here who's in a condition to work."

Glen fumbled to catch the expensive piece of equipment, then cradled it in his arms. "Um, sure, boss. Right away."

He didn't wait to see how Glen dealt with the model. Actually, he could care less if Glen led the model offstage with a carrot—make that an oxycontin—on a fucking stick. Instead, he fled into the quiet confines of his studio office, closed the door, and poured himself a drink at the bar. He sank into the leather recliner he kept there and stared up at the ceiling, wondering why he bothered working anymore. All he did was slam his head against a wall of frustration every time he stepped into the studio.

God knew it wasn't for the money. He had enough of that to last him several lifetimes.

It wasn't for the fame either. He was already one of the best known, most sought after photographers in the business. After fifteen years of struggle, heartache, and clawing his way up from rock bottom, he was sitting pretty at the top of the heap.

Why, then? Did he just have a masochistic streak? Did he enjoy the headaches and ulcers? Why did he continue to put himself through this torture?

The fucking little voice in his head, the one he could always count on to be brutally honest and never try to blow smoke up his ass, spoke up. *You know why.*

Okay, so maybe he did know. He just didn't want to admit it.

You keep doing it because you're still trying to prove yourself, to make sure people know you have value. To prove you aren't a useless, worthless omega.

Fucking inner voice. Right as always.

Trouble was, nobody he knew thought of him any way other than the filthy rich, famous, award-winning photographer who'd shot celebrities, movie stars, and fashion models for some of the most discerning magazines on the planet.

They knew him only as the man whose photos hung in exclusive galleries around the world and whose neatly matted prints sold for thousands of dollars each.

The people whose opinions he cared about, the ones he was still trying to impress, were back home in Appalachia, and they would no sooner pick up a copy of *Vogue* or *Cosmo* as they would try to set themselves on fire.

Maybe he should do a shoot for *Field and Stream.*

His annoying inner voice spoke up again. *Or maybe it's time to go home. They might be backward, but they're not Amish for God's sake. They read. They have satellite television. They must've heard about you.*

"Yeah, I doubt it." He swirled the liquor in his glass. "Even if they did hear about me, they'd think it had to be some other Mac Fuller. An omega couldn't possibly be a success." He took a sip of his scotch. "What qualifies someone as a success, anyway? Money? Power? Status? I've got all three, and I still feel like a worthless piece of shit sometimes." He sighed and let his head drop back, resting on the high back of the leather chair. The one thing I can be sure I am is an asshole, especially to Gary. Note to self: apologize and give Gary a bonus."

A chime sounded as an email landed in his inbox. He glanced at his phone, tempted to ignore it. He sipped his drink, staring at the highlighted number indicating he had a new unread email. Finally, he just rolled his eyes and reached over to pick up his phone. It might be important, like a new medication for drooping penis or some unknown Russian girls dying to send him photos of themselves.

It turned out the email was neither. It was from Cal Tech, from a B. Taylor. It took him a minute to figure out who B. Taylor might be and how he'd gotten Mac's private email. He finally remembered a scientist he'd met when he'd done a shoot on the Cal Tech campus. They'd had a few drinks together—okay, more than a few—and ended up in bed. Wasn't his name Barney? Or Barnaby? Something with a B. A more than half-decent lay, as Mac remembered, which was why he continued reading the email and didn't immediately hit delete since the last thing he needed was a one-night stand who wanted to be more.

Dear Mac,

How've you been? It's been a while since we last spoke, and I'm not referring to the few fevered grunts and groans and several rather emphatic, four-letter expletives we exchanged in your hotel suite. LOL.

I'm writing because of the conversation we had at the bar prior to all that. You'd mentioned coming from a rather remote area of the Appalachian Mountains in West Virginia. I've recently become involved in a mining project with interests in that general area and would like to pick your brain for information you may have that isn't readily available otherwise. Give me a call at your convenience.

Thanks, Blaine.

Blaine! Of course. That was his name. Now Mac remembered.

He drummed his fingers on the desk and took another sip of his drink. Now, this was interesting. A mining operation nosing around the pack's land? His lips tilted in a lopsided, mean little grin. The alphas would shit kittens if humans started mining anywhere *near* Wolf Valley. Mac would pay good money to see it too.

What the hell would anyone be mining for up there though? Coal companies had sniffed around the mountains sheltering Wolf Valley for decades, but no coal had ever been found up there. No oil, either, and not enough natural gas to make drilling cost effective. He also knew there wasn't enough gold in the mountain to fill a tooth.

In fact, there was nothing he could think of which would capture the interest of a mining company.

He was tempted to call Blaine and find out but decided against it. Even now, years after being cast out of the pack, he refused to give anyone information that might endanger pack privacy or safety.

Pathetic, thy name is Mac.

He compromised by saving the email. Maybe he'd change his mind about contacting Blaine later. You never knew.

The email had given him an itch, though. Maybe it *was* time to go back to Wolf Valley. God knew Mac could use a vacation. Besides, what had he done it for, clawed and fought to make a success of himself, if not to prove to the asshole alphas back home that he was as good—or better—than any of them? He could buy and sell them all twelve times over now. Maybe it was time for them to know it.

And while he was there, maybe he'd poke around a little and see if he could find out what was worth mining in the area. After all, although he already had a more than healthy portfolio, he was never one to pass up a solid investment.

THE SUV RENTAL ONLY TOOK him so far up the mountain before the terrain grew too overgrown for the vehicle to continue. He knew the pack used ATVs to ride the game trails down to the main road or chose to run on four feet through the forest, and as the SUV bounced hard over a particularly rough patch of ground, he remembered why. He pulled over and parked his vehicle where the road petered out into thickets of bushes and brambles. He locked it and stuffed the keys into his pocket. The only thing he carried was his camera equipment and a backpack with a change of clothes and a few toiletries. He'd be hiking as his man-self, which would take him a lot longer but would allow him to carry his precious camera, charger, and lenses. He went nowhere without them. Plus, he might get in a few good nature shots on the way.

He breathed in deep, drawing the scents of the mountain into his lungs. His wolf-self sprang to life within him, practically wriggling with happiness and excitement at the once-familiar odors. He could smell wildflowers, hickory nuts, and the rank smell of deer, small rodents, and bear. There was the tang of pine, the sweetness of birch. The earthy smell of dirt and the fresh scent of new grass almost masking the slightly musty, underlying smell of last year's growth. The air was also ripe with the spoor of both smaller animals—squirrel, rabbit, fox, possum, shrew—and larger predators like bear, bobcat, weasels, and of course, wolf.

This was home. This was where he belonged. If his tail had been in evidence, it would've been wagging.

His feet crunched on broken twigs and last year's deadfall as he made his way into the forest, navigating a deer trail that grew so steep in some areas he had to grab tree branches to help propel himself forward. He moved more or less northeast. Not that he was concerned about direction—getting lost wasn't even a possibility. Even after fifteen years, his soul knew the way home.

Hours passed as he walked. He grinned when he came to Jewel Creek. This far from the valley, it was just a thin dribble trickling over rocks, but he paused to scoop the cold, crystal water up in his hands and drink. It tasted like his past and brought a thick wealth of memories with it, not all of them unpleasant. He smiled wryly and then shot a few photos of the stream, closeups of the water splashing over the smooth rocks, before moving on.

The going became easier now that he had the stream to follow. The course of the water followed a relatively flat route, threading through the forest in winding, ever-widening line. Jewel Creek reached its widest point where the pack's settlement was built, measuring some twenty yards across and four feet deep at its center. The sun was well into its descent before he finally stood at the edge of the forest looking down into the cozy valley he'd once called home.

His first impression was that time had frozen the moment he'd left. Everything looked just as he remembered. The cabins still stood in a semicircle around the central clearing on the north bank of the creek, the larger, better appointed homes up front. The structures in each successive semicircle gradually reduced in size and quality, until the last group, which were no more than shabby shanties, some with tarpaper roofs, some with hammered tin. Perhaps there were a couple more cabins than he remembered, several more satellite dishes, and a newly shingled roof here and there, but ultimately, little of substance had changed. Alphas, betas, deltas, gammas, and omegas were still obviously segregated. Separate, but not at all equal. Nowhere was the disparity between the castes more blatantly apparent than in their homes' construction. Even amenities like satellite dishes were far more prevalent on the roofs of the alphas' homes, becoming fewer and farther between in the delta and gamma rows, and disappearing completely in the omega section.

Omegas. The hardest working members of the pack and yet still considered the lowest of the low.

He swallowed hard, then lifted his chin, straightened his spine, and summoned the pride he'd worked so hard to attain over the past fifteen years. He stood tall and strong as he strode into the heart of the settlement. People paused as he passed, staring at him through narrow eyes. Strangers were rare, possibly dangerous, and therefore, ultimately suspect. Mothers chased their children inside, casting worried glances in his direction. Men began gathering in small groups on porches, watching him with hard eyes. The smell of their fear and mistrust was thick in the air.

No one seemed to recognize him. He didn't know if he should be relieved or disappointed. A little of both, he decided. He knew he would never be allowed to continue to waltz freely through the camp completely unmolested, and was not looking forward to the moment of confrontation. He figured it would come as soon as the Alpha got wind of his presence. Word was probably winging its way toward the ear of the leader at light speed. It wouldn't be long now. His muscles tightened in readiness for a fight.

He threaded his way between cabins to the last row and then on to the final cabin, ignoring the hard stares aimed in his direction and the men who began following him. As he stepped up to the cabin, the door opened and a man, his hair and beard completely gray, face as weathered as old leather, walked outside. He was carrying a shotgun in the ready-for-business position.

"That'll be close enough, stranger. Who are you, and what do you want from us?"

Mac offered a smile but kept his eyes downcast in a wolfly gesture of respect. Direct eye contact would've been interpreted as hostile or aggressive. "Pa, it's me. It's McKenna."

Angus raised a bushy eyebrow and looked skeptical. "McKenna? *Our* Mac?" Angus lifted his chin and lowered the shotgun a bit. "You can't be him. My Mac is dead. Left in a snowstorm over a dozen years ago." The barrel came up again. "What are you trying to pull?"

So, they thought he was dead. It made sense. They would believe he'd perished because no omega could possibly be strong enough or smart enough to make it through the storm, not to mention fifteen years on their own in the world of the humans, least of all a Fuller. It hurt Mac that even his family believed it. "I hate to disappoint you, Pa, but I'm very much alive."

Angus blinked and cocked his head, looking at Mac askance, finally leaning in and taking a deep sniff of Mac's scent. Then his eyes widened, and he lowered the gun. "Mac? Is it really you?" He called back over his shoulder. "Sylva! Come out here. Our boy's come home!" He dropped the shotgun on the porch and, for the first time in fifteen years, embraced his son.

His ma looked as washed out and worn as an old dish-cloth when she pushed Angus out of the way and grabbed Mac's shoulders with surprisingly strong fingers. "Mac? Oh, lord, lord, you're alive!" She pulled him down and threw her arms around his neck. "We thought you was dead. All these years, believed you was gone! Where've you been all this time? Why didn't you let us know you were alive?" She pushed him away just as abruptly, sniffling loudly, her smile melting into a frown as she squeezed his biceps. "You've grown tall, but you ain't nothing but skin and bones. Don't they feed you where you been?"

Mac chuckled. "I'm not too skinny, Ma. I've been eating fine."

"Well, you look like a scrawny runt, but it makes no never mind. I'll fatten you up soon enough. Come on inside. Let me dish you up some stew. It's rabbit with fresh baked biscuits."

Before he could go inside, Angus suddenly grabbed the shotgun from the porch floor and stared over Mac's shoulder.

The group of men who'd followed Mac to the omega section of the settlement had quietly been gathering in front of the Fuller cabin. Now one of them spoke. "Hold on right there, stranger."

He turned and saw a familiar-looking man dressed in

worn jeans and a black Harley Davidson T-shirt smeared with streaks of grease. It took Mac a minute to realize it was Luc Alden, grown up and looking every bit as mean as Luc's father had.

It didn't take long to start matching names to the other faces, either. JJ Alden and Will Butten were there, and a few older men he remembered as well. Alphas, all of them. "It's me, Luc. McKenna."

"Yeah? So, I hear. Maybe I don't believe it."

Mac grunted and shrugged, and he could see by the narrowing of Luc's eyes how much his nonchalant dismissal of Luc's opinion irked. "Doesn't make it not true. Where's your father, Luc?"

"Dead." Luc suddenly seemed to remember who he was. He puffed out his chest and snarled. "I'm leader now, and I say you ain't no more McKenna than you are Elvis."

If Luc was leader, it wasn't by democratic election, Mac knew. Pack rule was decided by a fight between the current leader and a challenger. It wasn't usually to the death, but it often was. Luc must've fought and probably killed his own father to take over leadership of the pack.

"Well, um, congratulations, I guess."

Angus spoke up. "He's our Mac all right, Luc. A pa don't forget his son's scent."

Luc looked like he wanted to argue but couldn't seem to come up with a logical argument. Every wolf knew what Angus said was true. Wolves remembered scents, those of kin most of all. "Well, what do you know. What are you doing back here? You was banished, last I recall."

Mac nodded. "I know, but I thought—"

Luc guffawed and crossed his beefy arms over his chest. "Well, that there was your first mistake. Omegas *can't* think. They're too stupid. Everybody know that."

The men behind him snorted and laughed. "Ain't that the truth, Luc?"

Luc waited for the laughter to die down. "You best get going again before I decide to strip your hide from your bones, boy. Your banishment was forever. That means you don't never get to come back."

"I know what forever means." Mac scowled at them. "But I wasn't guilty of the crime I was banished for, and you know it, Luc."

"Seems I remember differently."

"Then you're remembering wrong." Angus placed a hand on his arm, but he shook it off. He'd lived among humans for fifteen years, grown up outside the pack. He'd acquired a different set of values and no longer believed alphas were better than or stronger than or smarter than anyone else. Moreover, he wasn't afraid to prove it. Not anymore. "You want me to leave? You'll have to make me this time. You and me, we'll have a go-round. Right here, right now."

The men behind Luc gasped, and Luc's eyes widened. To a man, they looked shocked, probably never having heard such audacity coming from an omega before. They certainly didn't expect one to stand up and challenge the leader of the pack at first glance, either. No one seemed to know how to handle the situation, especially since Angus McKenna was armed.

Mac pressed the issue. If Luc was the same cowardly asshole he'd been when he was young, then there was no way Luc would take Mac up on his offer—not when Luc had no chance to cheat and could possibly lose a fight and leadership of the pack in front of witnesses. "Well, Luc? You wanna go?"

"Aw, screw him, Luc." It was JJ. "He's only an omega. He ain't worth your time."

"Yeah, you're right. He ain't worth it." Luc spat at Mac's feet. "Stay if you want. You can work cutting timber with your old man." He turned and gestured toward the group of men. "Let's go."

Mac remained on the rickety porch, waiting until the group disappeared around the corner of the farthest cabin. Only when he was sure they weren't coming back did he drop his guard and relax a bit. He turned around and followed his mother inside.

He didn't feel like eating, although Sylva placed a steaming bowl of delicious-smelling stew in front of him. Nothing had changed since he'd left. The alphas still thought he was worthless, not even worth the energy it would take to throw him out. They didn't know about his accomplishments and didn't care how hard he'd worked or how much he'd sacrificed to earn his success. To them, he was still an insignificant, ignorant omega who could barely think clearly enough to tie his own boots.

Fine.

If that's all they expected of him, then that's exactly what he'd give them, along with a heaping helping of attitude and a nice hard fist to chase it down their fucking throats.

I guess they aren't the only ones who haven't changed.

His lips curled in an amused smile, and his appetite suddenly revived, he picked up a spoon and tucked into the stew.

CHAPTER 2

I f there was one thing Blue Standish couldn't tolerate, it was a coward. It seemed to him cowardice was the seed from which all other faults grew. Liars, thieves, bullies, abusers...they all had wide yellow streaks running down their backs.

In his opinion, a man was a man when he owned up to his failures and worked hard to overcome them. A man made a living, took care of his family, lent a hand to his neighbors, and helped the less fortunate.

Luc Alden was practically the definition of the word "coward" in Blue's eyes. Oh, in the beginning, back when they were kids, he'd been enamored of Luc, just like practically all the other pack pups. Luc's father was the leader, and that made Luc the closest thing to a prince the pack had. Everybody practically tripped over themselves to get close to Luc, to earn his favor, even Blue. They'd do anything Luc told them to do to stay in his circle of friends, and continued to do so even as they'd grown older.

Blue had too. Right up until the day the omega boy died.

It'd been a cold day, he remembered, one of the bitterest

of the year by far. The smell of snow was heavy in the air, and the sky was filling with fat storm clouds. A big one was on the way, maybe the first real blizzard of the season. The Alpha Ones—that's what the pack's group of alpha teens called themselves—were out on the mountainside, hanging around, not doing much of anything except smoking some weed Luc had stolen from an older cousin's stash and trash talking the rest of the pack. They were bored and knew things would only get more boring once the storm hit. When the big snows blew across the valley, they'd all be restricted to their cabins, going no farther than the center of the village for most of the winter. Deep snow kept even the strongest wolves in their dens.

They'd been debating whether they wanted to shift and take a stab at hunting some rabbit or squirrel before it started to snow, when someone practically stumbled into their midst. It was an omega, and things suddenly got a whole lot more interesting.

Blue recognized the guy from the settlement. He thought the guy's name was Mark or Mike or something close. *Mac,* he thought. McKenna. That was it. One of the Fullers. Real cute guy. Tall with a fringe of sandy hair always in desperate need of a cut that continually fell in front of his crystal blue eyes. Nice body, strong and lean. Great ass.

Blue ducked his head and blushed, as if his friends could read his mind. Wolves, particularly alpha wolves, didn't think that way about *any* guy, let alone an omega. He didn't know what Luc would do to him if his secret was caught out, but it wouldn't be pretty, of that much Blue was sure.

It was common knowledge Mac had skirmishes with the boys of the Alpha Ones before, although Blue hadn't been present for any of them, but it looked to him like that was about to change. He felt a fight brewing; animosity was crackling in the air like static electricity.

He watched from under his eyelashes as Luc slowly circled Mac. He could almost see the hostility sizzling between the two. As a whole, alphas were not fond of omegas, didn't socialize with them, looked down on them, but few were as openly antagonistic toward them as the Alden family. Blue didn't know why, but the Aldens actively *hated* the omegas, and the Fuller clan in particular. Whatever the reason, An Alden never passed on the opportunity to give an omega, especially a Fuller, a beat down.

"What the fuck are you doing in my woods, omega?" Luc walked close to Mac and shoulder-bumped him. "Who gave you permission to come here? Best answer me if you want to keep your tongue in your head."

Mac looked down, but his cheeks burned red and he muttered an answer under his breath. "Nothing. Woods don't belong to just you."

Blue's eyes widened. Omegas rarely talked back to alphas, and never with belligerence. They were always respectful, usually using one-word sentences whenever possible.

Luc seemed as shocked as Blue. "What the fuck did you just say?"

"It's called Wolf Valley, ain't it? I'm a wolf too."

"You want me to rip your tongue out and nail it to the wall of your pa's cabin?"

"Well, you can try." Mac kept his eyes averted, but his tone was no less hostile. Then, to Blue's shock, Mac lifted his head and locked gazes with Luc.

The group of alphas hissed a collected gasp. Never mind Mac's insolence. That shocked them enough, but his body language went beyond even that. It was unheard of, practically a challenge for anyone to look an alpha in the eyes except for another alpha. It was the epitome of defiance. Mac couldn't have insulted Luc more if he'd pissed on Luc's shoes.

Blue had to disguise a laugh as a cough when Luc looked

27

away first. What the fuck was going on here? An omega just stared down an alpha! Then again, it just confirmed what Blue was beginning to believe—Luc, alpha or not, was a coward at heart. For the first time in his life, Blue looked at an omega as someone who might have potential.

Although Luc tried to cover up his act of submission by finding something intensely fascinating on a nearby tree limb, trying to pretend Mac wasn't worth his interest, Blue wasn't fooled. An alpha had just conceded a dominance challenge, however small, to an omega. Blue knew he'd never look at Luc quite the same way again.

Luc recovered quickly enough and rounded back on Mac. He took another tact as if trying to throw Mac off-balance. "What's that you got there? What are you holding behind your back?"

"Nothing." Mac was sullen but continued to stand his ground. Blue warmed with something close to respect for him. It must've taken a lot of courage for an omega to stand up to an alpha, particularly the son of the leader, especially without anyone to back him up.

"Bullshit." Luc signaled to JJ, who grabbed the object out of Mac's hands and gave it to Luc. "A camera? Look at this piece of shit!" He laughed and turned it around in his hands. "All busted up. Bet it don't even work." A contemptuous snarl curled his lip. "What do you do with this thing? Run around the forest pretending to take pictures?"

JJ and Will cracked up, howling with laughter as if what Luc said was the funniest thing they'd ever heard. "Yeah, Luc, that's what he does. Then he goes home and has pretend tea parties with his invisible playmates."

"Give it back!" Mac bared his teeth, a sign of aggression Blue couldn't ever remember seeing on an omega's face before. They were always so complacent, so docile, it was hard to believe Mac was one of them.

In a lightning quick move, Luc backhanded Mac. The sound was as sharp as a crack of thunder, and the look quickly coloring Mac's face was just as black as storm clouds.

"I'll fucking teach you to talk back to an alpha!" Luc snorted and lifted his arm as if to dash the camera on the ground when something no one would've ever expected to happen, did.

Mac charged Luc.

Blue gasped as Mac hurled himself on Luc, knocking Luc to the ground. The camera flew and landed at Blue's feet. Luckily, a mound of dead leaves broke its fall. Blue hardly noticed—his attention was riveted on the unbelievable fight going on right before his eyes.

Mac hammered Luc, raining down one blow after another. Luc heaved upward, and they rolled, but he didn't stay on top long before Mac had him on his back again. The two of them shifted into their wolf-selves at almost the same time, and the fight got bloody. Both snarled and bit wherever they could, but it was clear Mac was winning. In the end, it took both JJ and Will to pull Mac off Luc. Blue was pretty sure Mac would've killed Luc if they hadn't finally intervened.

When he shifted back into his man-form, Luc's nose was dripping blood and his eyes were beginning to swell shut. Purplish bruises were already blooming on his face. One ear was bleeding profusely. "You fucking bastard! You're dead! You hear me? Dead! You and your whole fucking family!" He limped away, followed by JJ, Will, and the others. Only Blue remained behind.

Blue bit his lip, torn between running after the other alphas and staying to help Mac. He took a couple of steps in the direction Luc had led the gang, then paused. He turned back toward Mac. "You okay?"

He didn't look okay, although he was nowhere near in as

bad shape as Luc had been. It was clear to Blue who won the fight, and it hadn't been the alpha. According to pack law, Mac should be the new leader of the group, but it didn't look as if Luc was going to abide by the rules.

Blue was still very young, and he'd never been in a situation like it before. He didn't know what to do or how to respond. Should he follow the established alpha or stand with the new leader?

Mac didn't seem to care. He grimaced as he gingerly felt the swelling under his eye, and turned his back on Blue. He picked up his camera, cradled it to his chest, and walked away.

After a moment spent staring at Mac's back as he disappeared into the forest, Blue followed Luc and the Alpha Ones.

Later, he watched the confrontation between Mac and Luc's father, Gray Alden, and the other alpha adult members of the pack with dismay. Lies! They were telling lies. When Gray banished Mac, Blue cringed.

Banishment was as good as a death sentence for an omega. Everybody knew it. They couldn't survive on their own without the pack. What had Mac done to deserve it? He was telling the truth—Luc had started the fight. Besides, Mac won! He should be leader of the Alpha Ones now, not banished. It was Luc who should be disgraced by pack law.

Blue knew the truth, but he couldn't bring himself to intervene in pack business, especially not in defense of an omega, and particularly not when it would be in direct conflict with the pack leader. What would everyone say? What if he got banished too? Fear made the choice for him. Then guilt began to weigh him down, but he remained quiet anyway.

In that moment, he'd recognized his own spinelessness was born out of fear, and had been more disgusted with himself and mortified by his inaction than he'd ever been before or since. He'd become the one thing he couldn't abide —a coward. As he'd watched Mac run off toward the forest carrying nothing but that old dilapidated camera, he'd resolved to never tolerate cowardice ever again, not in others and certainly not in himself.

It was a promise that'd cost him, but one he'd managed to keep for the next fifteen years.

* * *

LIFE WASN'T the same for Blue after Mac was banished. Time passed, and he grew older, but whether he grew any wiser was up for debate. He went to school with the other alphas (even in school, the pack members were segregated by caste), and learned to read, write, and cipher. Pack school terminated at twelfth grade for alphas, although it ended four years earlier for everyone else. The pack thinking was gammas, deltas, and especially omegas didn't need an education past the eighth-grade level. In fact, few omegas even made it *that* far.

By the time Blue graduated, he'd grown six inches taller and his frame filled out, becoming more muscular, transitioning from boy to man. His wolf-self grew too—he was large, lean, and healthy, with a thick, shaggy gray coat. But the biggest changes had come on the inside.

As he matured, he began to question the very structure of pack order and, as a result, distanced himself from the other alphas. He stayed at home more and more when he wasn't hunting, finding comfort in books. Whenever he got his hands on cash money, he would beg a trip down to the human village where a small used bookshop waited. He'd come home with a bagful of books and spend the next couple of weeks working his way through them. Then he'd reread them, until he had the money to make another trip to the village.

He didn't roam the hillsides with the Alpha Ones anymore, either. After a while, they stopped asking him to go, and ignored him. He found he liked it better that way, but his reticence was being noticed by more than his friends. His ma and pa noticed and weren't happy with the changes they saw in him.

It came to a head one night shortly after he turned twenty-one.

"You're an alpha, Blue, but you don't go to the meetings, don't run with your friends anymore. Folks are sayin' you're acting mighty peculiar." His mother, Irvina, placed a steaming bowl of venison stew on the table in front of him. "It ain't proper, Blue."

"Ma, this is nothing for you to worry on. I don't care what people say. I'm happy doing my own thing."

"No, your ma is right, Blue. You're a grown man now, not a pup anymore. It's past time for you to take an interest in pack dealings." His father, Argyle, sat at the kitchen table and broke off a piece of fresh-baked bread from a thick slice. "As an alpha, it's your responsibility to be a leader." After dunking the bread in the stew, he stuck it in his mouth and chewed.

"Why, Pa?"

Argyle looked up, his bushy gray brows knitting. "Why, what?"

"Why is the alphas' responsibility to lead, to hunt? What makes us so all-fired smart? What puts us above the deltas, gammas, and omegas?"

Irvina gasped and placed a hand on her chest. She glanced around the kitchen with wide eyes, as if worried someone might've overheard what Blue said. "Why are you talking this way, Blue? You catch a fever?"

"No, I'm not sick. I'm just wondering, that's all, Ma. Seems to me there's no difference between us all except—"

His pa interrupted him. "Stop this crazy talk. Got your nose in them books too much. That's what I think. Now, eat your supper."

"But Pa—"

Argyle's hand slammed down on the table hard enough to rattle the bowls and silverware. Stew slopped over the rim of his bowl, splattering the pretty lace tablecloth. "Enough! Are you trying to rile me, boy? You ain't too big for me to take you outside and cut a switch. I don't care how old you are. You ain't gonna disrespect me, or our pack, not at my table. I'm still your father!"

Blue shook his head. "No, Pa. I don't mean any disrespect. Honest. I've just been thinking on it a lot lately, and—"

"Well, that's your trouble, then. You think too much. Always have. Smarter folks than us made the rules. Ain't our place to question them. Now, there'll be no more talk like this in my house, hear? You want to think? Then ponder on going to pack meetings and doing your duty as an alpha. In fact, it's time you started thinking about mating. Pick a girl, get hitched, give me and your ma a litter of grandpups. Give you something to do 'sides think and read your books." Argyle dunked the rest of the hunk of bread into the stew and stuffed it into his mouth. He turned to his wife, an obvious signal the conversation with his son was at an end. He spoke around a mouthful of bread. "The gammas give you any of them beans they put up for the winter, Irvina?"

She glanced sideways at Blue but nodded. "Yes, dear. And I got our share of the pickled tomatoes too."

"Good. Gonna have to get an omega to shore up our woodpile. It's a little low. Those clouds look belly-heavy with snow. I don't want to have to trek all the way to the omega cabins in a blizzard to get wood if we run out."

Blue stared at the stew, his appetite gone. Were his parents really as blind as the rest of the pack? Did no one ever question why there were such strict lines between the pack members? Was he really the only one? Did that mean there was something wrong with him? Or was there something screwy with everyone else? It all seemed so...so arbitrary to him. There wasn't any good reason—hell, any reason *at all*—for the caste system in the pack. And it was crazy how everyone went along with it, especially the omegas. Why did they allow themselves to be treated this way?

Maybe he was the crazy one. He *felt* normal -- confused and cynical, but normal. He just couldn't bring himself to live by rules he no longer believed in, but where did that leave him? He couldn't run away. No other pack would accept a rogue alpha wolf. A delta or gamma, sure. Packs could always use more of them. Even a runaway omega might be taken in, if the pack was short workers, but an alpha? Someone who might someday challenge for leadership? Never.

Could he live among the humans? He wouldn't even know where to begin to pass as a human, and there was no one here he trusted enough to ask. He'd been to the human city, of course, many times, but his contact with them had been extremely limited. He'd go in, buy his books, and leave everything else to the older wolves, his pa included. They were the ones to do the talking and trading.

All he did know was, no matter what his father ordered to the contrary, he had a lot of thinking to do.

He was still thinking about it when the past strolled into the settlement, full of attitude and swagger and looking like sex on a stick.

CHAPTER 3

Blue thrust fingers into his hair, pushing the longer strands off his forehead, then slanted his hand over his eyes, shading them from the glaring sun. He was standing on the porch of his cabin looking out toward Jewel Creek, watching for the stranger to reappear. Several minutes passed before he finally spotted the lone figure ambling alongside the stream.

Except it wasn't really a stranger. Incredibly, folks said it was McKenna Fuller come back from the dead. Blue had never seen a ghost, didn't really believe in them, but the man he saw wandering along the stream sure appeared to be one. At least, that's what some folks were saying.

A closer look proved it was Mac Fuller, all right, and all signs indicated he was very much alive. Blue remembered the stubborn tilt and deep cleft in his chin and those piercing blue eyes. Somehow, Mac had survived the banishment all those years ago. Now he'd returned to Wolf Valley all grown up. Blue's eyesight was keen, and from what he was seeing, Mac Fuller had matured from a cute teen into six feet or so of badass sexy. The way he filled out the jeans he was wearing was downright criminal.

The story of how Mac stared down Luc Alden yesterday at Fuller cabin was spreading all over the settlement and growing more incredible with every telling. People flat-out couldn't believe it, even those who'd seen it with their own eyeballs. It was all everyone was talking about, even Blue's ma and pa. In their experience, no omega had the balls to stand up to an alpha, let alone the leader. And never had anyone come back once they were banished. Some said the story was a lie; the others insisted it was true, and it proved their theory that Mac was a ghost. Only a ghost would have no fear of the alpha killing them for such insolence.

Other folks might not believe the tale, but Blue did. After all, he'd seen Mac go head-to-head with Luc before and win, back when they were barely more than pups. It was why Mac had been banished from Wolf Valley to begin with. Now he'd come back fully grown, a tall, powerful man. Blue didn't doubt for one minute that Mac had taken Luc on again.

Not that Luc was a strong leader, anyway. He was all bite and bark and no goddamn common sense. As bad as his father had been, Luc was ten times worse. He was a mean, lazy, arrogant coward and a discredit to his bloodline, in Blue's opinion. The Wolf Valley pack would be better off with a different leader, for sure, and the sooner the better. Not that there was anyone around eager to challenge Luc.

Blue shivered, remembering the bloodbath following Luc's succession as leader. Luc planned the fight for months before challenging his father. When he called people to witness the fight, Blue had come running with the rest of the pack. Gray answered the challenge but looked shaky and weak, as if sick. Blue had wondered many times since the fight if Luc poisoned Gray before making the challenge. It made sense to Blue. Luc was a dirty fighter and had never won a fair fight in his life.

Luc had Gray on his back in no time flat. It hadn't been a clean, easy death for Gray. No quick bite to the throat. It seemed as if Luc wanted it to last, bleeding Gray out a bit at a time. Gray's death was ugly and brutal, and more than one pack member looked away long before Gray breathed his last.

As soon as Gray Alden lay dead on the ground, while his blood still soaked the dirt, Luc and his cronies, JJ and Will, along with a few others—all of whom had been members of the Alpha Ones in their teens—had systematically attacked and killed anyone who even *looked* like they might challenge Luc's claim to leadership.

No one expected the attack, and none were prepared for it. Five alphas, all relatives of Luc, joined Gray Alden on the blood-sodden earth by the time it was all said and done. Luc wasted no time giving the surviving adult female spouses and daughters as mates to alpha men who had none, or who wanted a second wife. Any unwanted females were first offered to the deltas, then gammas, and finally if no one wanted her, she was demoted to omega and sent to the outermost circle of cabins to live or die at the charity of the omegas. Luc and his friends divvied up the dead alphas' cabins and possessions for themselves. Spoils of war, Luc called them.

As for most of the dead alphas' children, well… Blue didn't like to think about what happened to them. Everyone knew life in the wild could be harsh for wolf pups. Not all survived into adulthood, right? That's what his ma and pa told him, but he couldn't bring himself to believe it. They weren't wild wolves, dammit! There was more to the pack than that. There was human in them, although no one in the pack ever wanted to admit it.

Still, He'd never seen such insane viciousness before or since. He'd tried to stop the Alpha Ones, he truly had, and his hide bore the scars to prove it, but he couldn't save the children. Only the intervention of his father and uncles kept Luc from killing Blue that day. He'd hated Luc even more intensely afterward.

Blue growled and put Luc Alden out of his mind. He turned his attention back to the solitary figure walking along the stream. It was time to find out just where McKenna Fuller had been all these years, how he'd survived, and most of all, why Mac had come back to Wolf Valley.

Long strides brought him across the wide clearing to the stream, and he hurried to catch up to Mac, who was almost to the tree line. "Hey, Mac! Wait up."

Mac glanced back at him. An expression of surprise morphed into a frown as Blue approached.

"Hey. Remember me? I'm Blue—"

"Yeah, I know who you are, Standish. What are you doing out here without Luc and the others? I thought you Alpha One boys didn't wipe your asses without each other."

Blue gaped at Mac in shock. What sort of omega *was* this? Who disrespected an alpha right off the bat without even a greeting? No one Blue had ever known, for sure. "I… I don't spend much time with Luc anymore, or with the Alpha Ones. None, actually, if I can help it."

"Oh?"

He shook his head. "Yeah. Luc's a vicious asshole." *Oh my Lord! Did I say that out loud?* It was difficult to fight the urge to clamp his hand over his mouth in horror. "Besides, you know, he's a little busy now, being the leader of the pack and all."

Mac snorted. "Yeah, I think you got it right the first time. He was an asshole before I left. Now he's just a bigger, older, uglier one. Guess some things never change."

Blue cocked his head. "You didn't change much either, did you? You're an omega, but you never acted like one. Still don't. You've got more balls than ever, from what I hear."

"Yeah, well, where I've been living, things are different than they are here." He turned to walk away, but Blue kept pace with him. He stopped again and looked at Blue. "Where are you going?"

Blue was taken aback again. Omegas would never question an alpha like this, but instead of irritating him, it fueled his curiosity about Mac. "With you. For a walk, I guess."

"Didn't say I wanted company."

"That's fine, but I don't remember asking you. It's a free forest."

"Have it your way." Mac sniffed but didn't question him anymore. They walked in silence for a few minutes before Blue picked up the conversation again. "How were things different?"

"What?"

"You said things were different where you'd been living. Did you get another pack to take you in?" Blue's curiosity sharpened, demanding to be satisfied.

"No. The last thing I wanted was to join another pack and go through the same bullshit all over again, even if I could find one willing to take me in."

"So, where did you go?"

"Into the human city. A lot of cities, actually."

Blue's eyes popped open wide. Could the rumors actually be true? He found it amazing and fascinating. "You lived with the humans? For real? What city? Like, New York?"

"There, sure. Chicago. Dallas. Los Angeles of late. I travel a lot. Been to almost every big city in the United States and a bunch of the smaller ones. I spent some time in Paris and London, Berlin, and Hong Kong too. Lived almost six months in Tokyo."

They reached the tree line and began an easy hike through the forest, still following Jewel Creek. The forest closed behind them, screening them from the rest of the settlement. Blue felt relieved once no one could see him walking with an omega any longer, then immediately felt ashamed for feeling that way. Why should he care who saw him walking with Mac. Even if Mac was an omega, weren't they all the same pack? Why did the rest of the alphas find it so distasteful?

Blue didn't know whether he truly believed Mac or not though. On the surface it sounded to him like Mac was spinning tall tales, but then again, a pup surviving in winter without the support of the pack and growing up in the outside world among humanity was astonishing, too. But Mac's presence, alive and well proved it could be done, as incredible as it seemed. There was no other explanation for Mac's existence other than what was purported. Blue reluctantly decided that, as unlikely as it seemed, Mac was telling the truth. "What was it like, living with the humans?"

Mac shrugged. "Hard, especially in the beginning when I young. If you think living in the mountains is hard, try doing it on the streets of a human city." His chin tipped up in what was probably an unconscious sign of pride. "I made it though. I survived."

"I can see that, and while I'm surprised, I'm also impressed."

Turning on him, Mac growled. "Surprised? Impressed? Why? Because I'm a worthless omega?"

Blue frowned and shook his head. "No. Because you're a wolf, and they're human. You grew up here, with me, and I know I wouldn't have had the first clue how to survive in the human world."

Color flushed in Mac's cheeks, and he ducked his head as if embarrassed. "Oh."

He bit back a smile and decided to let Mac have a free pass. "I mean, it couldn't have been easy. How did you shift? Where did you run? How did you hunt?"

Mac grunted and shrugged. "It was difficult finding places to shift and run, especially in the cities. I had to stay in the shadows, avoid being seen. I shifted and ran through the sewer systems mostly. Man, those places stank to high heaven. You wouldn't believe the stench. You know the stank of the cesspit? This is that many times over. I could barely breathe sometimes, especially in summer. Even above ground stank with exhaust fumes and sewer lines. I ran when I had to, but I tried to stay inside in the air-conditioning whenever I could."

Blue shivered. He hated going anywhere near the cesspit, the deep hole where the omegas would dump the contents of the outhouses when they were filled. Every spring, the omegas would dig a new pit and sprinkle lime dust on the old one to combat the smell, but the stink never really subsided, not for a long, long time. "I've only been off the mountain a few times and never to a really big city, but the ones I've been to smelled pretty bad too." Blue cocked his head. "Is that what you meant by it being different from here?"

"Partially, but the real difference are the people. They aren't segregated out there, at least not in most places. Oh, there are poor people and rich people, good people and bad, ambitious and lazy, sure, but no one stops a man from trying to change or to better himself."

"Huh." Blue didn't know if he believed that either. He decided to change the subject. "So, what are you going to do now that you're home? Even better, why did you come back at all?"

Blue's expression hardened for a minute. "My reasons are my own." Then he shrugged. "I guess I'll cut timber with my dad while I'm here. After all, that's what the *leader* ordered me to do." He spat the word like it was poison in his mouth. Mac scowled again and turned on Blue. "Which reminds me, *you're* an alpha. Why are you bothering with an omega like me?"

His chin went up out of habit. "I can spend time with whoever I want."

"Yeah, well, too bad I don't have the same right."

Blue couldn't really dispute it. He knew it was the truth. "I don't agree with pack law on everything."

Mac's lip curled over his teeth. "Oh, you don't agree? Well, that makes it all right then."

"Hey, no need to get hostile—"

"Look, I gotta get back. There's wood to be cut. Chores to be done. Asses to be wiped." Mac tossed Blue a look that was colder than any blizzard wind and turned on his heel. He headed off back the way they'd come, leaving Blue staring after him, feeling more confused than ever.

What had just happened? They'd been getting on fine. At least, Blue *thought* they had, but then... Pow! Mac exploded and ran off.

Well, he didn't exactly run. He more or less stalked away. Blue headed back as well, albeit at a much slower pace than Mac, replaying their encounter in his mind. *He got angry, but all I did was ask why he came back and what he was going to do now that he had. I just don't get it. Does he ever act like he's supposed to?*

The obvious answer was no. In fact, he was fairly certain Mac had never acted like an omega, *ever*.

Blue's lips twitched into a smile. *I was right about one thing though—he really does have a fine ass.*

Just then a thought occurred to him, and he broke into a run, dashing through the wood until he caught up to Mac. "Wait a minute! Mac, hold up!"

Mac paused but obviously wasn't happy about it. "What?"

"I have a job for you."

"What do you mean?"

"I don't know if you remember, but my family runs the logging business for the pack. While you were away, we started cutting timber to sell down in the city to the humans. It brings in extra cash for stuff we can't grow or make ourselves."

"Yeah, I noticed all the new satellite dishes. Except on the omega cabins, I mean."

Blue frowned. Although Mac's words weren't hostile, his voice was heavy with sarcasm. Blue chose to ignore it. Again. "I just figured maybe I could get you a job working for the company. I mean, your family can probably use the money, right?"

"I don't need charity."

"That's not what this is!"

"Yeah? Your family is in the habit of hiring omegas?"

Mac struck a nerve and Blue's hackles went up. It was true. His family didn't hire omegas unless they were short workers, preferring to have deltas and gammas on the payroll, and when they *did* hire omegas, it was usually for less money and for the dirtiest, most dangerous jobs, but he wasn't about to admit to it. "You know, you can be quite an asshole. I'm trying to be nice here!"

Mac's gaze bore into him, and it was all he could do to return the stare and not look away. Damn it, he wished Mac would stop acting so un-omega-like. It was constantly disconcerting. He also wished he could figure out why he was trying so hard to be nice to Mac. He didn't owe Mac a goddamn thing, did he? Yet here he was, practically begging Mac to take a job. Why? Why didn't he just walk away and leave Mac to whatever fate had in store?

43

Because you didn't stand up for him when it counted, and you've felt guilty ever since. That's why.

Damn his conscience. He really wished it would shut up and leave him the fuck alone.

"Okay, I'll do it."

"Huh? You will?" Blue blinked. "Um, okay then. I'll arrange it."

"Yeah. But not because I need the money. I just want to see how the timber business works."

"Um, okay—"

Mac turned and stalked away again, Blue's gaze following him.

Oh yeah, he thought, as his body reacted to the sight of Mac's firm ass hitching hypnotically under the worn denim. *I don't care why he wants the job, because now I remember another reason why I'm being so nice. It's because I admire that very fine caboose he's got, and if he's working for me, I get to see it every day.*

This time, he ignored the voice of his conscience when it started bitching at him.

CHAPTER 4

The logging operation owned by the Standish clan ran like a well-oiled machine—for the most part. Everyone had their job, everyone did their job, and nobody went home until said job was put to bed.

Tempers between workers flared, though, and often. Fights broke out, always delta against delta or gamma against gamma, never failing to slow production, much to the dismay and frustration of the Standish family. Blue's father and uncle, the owners of the Standish logging company, never seemed to agree on why.

Blue's father, Argyle, and his uncle, Enoch, argued about it all the time, and everyone in the pack had heard stories of the two Standish brothers' fights. Mac's father had mentioned it over supper the night before, when he heard Mac was going to work for them.

"Have a care, McKenna. Don't get between 'em when they start to fighting. You'll get bit for sure." Then Angus told the story of the last time they'd fought. Which, as it turned out, was just a few days ago.

"See, Enoch was up there at the camp, pushing his point,

jabbing his bony finger at the window. Busser Mathews was there, and I heard the story straight from him. Said Enoch was working himself up into fine lather about the all the fights the workers got theirselves into.

"Enoch says to Argyle, 'They're fighting all the time. Well, who can blame them? The work is beneath them, against their nature. How many times have I told you? It ought be the omegas out there, swinging the axes. Save us a bunch of money in wages too. We'd only need to pay them, what? Half what we pay the others?'"

Sylva laughed and passed Mac a basket of fresh baked rolls. "I can just hear ol' Enoch saying it too. All bluster, no bite, that one."

Angus shook his head. "Don't you believe it. Enoch is old, but he ain't stupid. He's more like a copperhead than a wolf. Hiding in plain sight, ready to strike when a person ain't looking, and twice as deadly as a full-on attack."

"Oh, pshaw." Sylva waved a hand at Angus. "Go on, finish tellin' your story."

"Well, Argyle would sooner fall over dead than agree with anything Enoch says. Busser says Argyle said, 'Bullshit. Ain't nothing wrong with deltas or gammas working up a sweat. It ain't like we got alphas working up here, for God's sake.' Seems Argyle thinks there's something out there on the mountain, some aller...allergi..."

"Allergen?" Mac offered.

"Yeah! That's the word. Allergen. Argyle thinks it's some mold or spores or such making the wolves fight. 'Course, then Enoch just blew a raspberry and called Argyle an idiot. Then Argyle called Enoch a senile ol' bastard, and the argument ramped up a notch. Next thing you know, Busser says the fight was on. Argyle and Enoch went at each other, spilling out of the office and across the logging compound. Now, neither one is a young pup, so the fight was just as quick to end as it was to start, with both of them gasping for air and slinking off to lick their wounds." Angus slapped his knee and guffawed. "Imagine, a pair of grown alphas fighting like school pups, rolling around in the dirt. I tell you, I'd pay good money to see it."

So far, Mac hadn't seen much at all, except for trees and sour expressions on the faces of the delta and gamma lumberjacks he'd followed up the mountain.

The overseer on shift today was a gruff delta with a head full of iron-gray hair and a full grizzled beard. He moved like molasses dripping from a spoon in winter, but he had sharp eyes despite his age and missed nothing. He carried a walking stick fashioned from black cherry, the handle carved with a wolf head, and used it to poke and prod workers he felt needed motivation, which was quite often, in Mac's opinion.

"You! New guy." He sniffed the air around Mac and wrinkled his nose as if he'd smelled something rancid. "You reek of omega. What are you doing up here?"

Another man, not quite as gray as the overseer, but not far from it, approached. Mac saw a familial resemblance to Blue in the man's face and guessed it was Argyle. With the realization a dim, hazy memory surfaced of Argyle standing beside Gray Alden on the day Mac was banished. "Smithy, have you seen my brother?"

"No, sir. Haven't seen Mr. Enoch this morning."

"If you do, tell him I'm looking for him. Now, leave this man be, Smithy. Blue hired him on."

"But he's an omega, Mr. Standish! We don't hire omegas for this operation." Smithy huffed and poked at Mac with his walking stick. "They're lazy, worthless—"

"My boy wants him on, so he's on. Mind your place, Smithy. You ain't irreplaceable neither. Now, let's move." He kicked a mound of wood shavings with his foot. "I want all this slash cleaned up by sundown. Damn shit catches like a cold. We don't need a fire on the mountain."

Smithy growled but nodded and jabbed the end of his stick at Mac again. "You heard Mr. Standish! Move along with you!"

Mac showed incredible restraint, in his opinion, by not taking the walking stick and stuffing it up Smithy's wrinkled old ass. Instead, he grunted almost imperceptibly as he hefted a large, heavy bundle of twigs and small branches to his shoulder and carried it off toward the wood chipper.

The chipper ground the timber slash into tiny pieces, which were bagged and sold to the power plant down in the human city for use in the production of electricity or heat, or so he'd been told that morning when he'd shown up for work. Slash made excellent tinder, and left strewn on the mountainside, a stray spark or lightning strike could send the whole area up in flames.

He still wasn't sure why he'd taken the job Blue offered him. His hefty savings were just sitting idle in the banks back home, growing fatter by the day, collecting interest and dividends from his investments. He certainly didn't need to haul lumber or cut timber for the Standish clan for the paltry paycheck they offered. The only reason he could think of for taking the job was his father and mother. When word reached them about the offer, they were so excited they swelled up with pride.

"Imagine, an omega working on the Standish logging operation!" His pa had beamed, strutting like a rooster. "And a Fuller, at that!"

His mother baked a pie with one of the last jars of her canned apples and presented it to Mac as if it were made of gold. For her, it was. They were only rationed a certain amount of fruit and needed to stretch it to see them through the winter. Using an entire jar in a pie was a rare and costly extravagance.

He could've just told them. "Ma, Pa, I'm rich. So rich you wouldn't believe it. I can buy you anything you want. Build you a house anywhere in the world."

Except he knew, just *knew*, they wouldn't believe him.

Because no omega ever got rich. No omega was ever successful. Ever.

Anyway, he didn't have the heart to dim the light shining in his parents' eyes. Even though he hadn't been at fault and was hurt by their refusal to stand up for him back when he'd been banished, they were still his parents, and he loved them. He'd taken the job for now, until he could figure out a way to convince his kin neither he nor they needed to be pack workhorses any longer.

It wasn't proving to be an easy choice. Physically, the work was exhausting. Each morning he'd get up at the first hint of sunrise to help his father cut timber for the pack's personal use. Then, after breakfast, he'd hurry to the Standish cabin and hitch a ride on one of their ATVs up to the logging camp. If he couldn't score a ride, he would hike up on foot. Eight or ten hours later, dirty and exhausted, stinking of sweat and sticky with sap, he'd start walking back home. It was often full dark before he made it back.

Mentally, it was even more tiring. Frustrating too.

No one seemed to believe he was supposed to be on the crew. They all gave him sideways glances and talked about him as if he was invisible. Nothing they said was complimentary either.

It was obvious nobody wanted to work with him. The other men kept their distance, and he was only given jobs he could do alone—such as picking up and bundling the slash. A gamma would take his load and run it through the chipper—they didn't trust an omega to run the expensive machinery.

One afternoon during their lunch break, Mac sat apart from the others as usual, his back against a tree. His lunch pail was open, and he was chewing on a strip of jerky. Suddenly, a younger man, a delta who sat with a few other workers on the other side of a small clearing, called out to him.

"Hey, omega! Go fetch us some water from the creek."

Mac ignored him and continued to eat his lunch. He was nobody's errand boy, and quite frankly, he was getting sick and tired of the attitudes of the other workers. Fuckers, one and all.

"Didn't you hear me? You deaf or just stupid?" The other workers chuckled and catcalled. "I said go fetch us some water."

Instead, Mac took a long pull from his canteen. The cool water slid down his throat but did nothing to extinguish the growing anger burning in his belly.

Looking back, it might not have been the brightest idea he'd ever had. Baiting the delta was a bad move for an omega, because no one would ever fight with him or even *side* with him if push came to shove. Which, when the delta got up and stalked across the clearing toward Mac, it quickly did.

The delta—Mac thought his name might've been Rick or Dick or something similar—growled at him. "You're that asshole who got banished, ain't you? What, you been gone so long you forgot your place, huh? I'll be real happy to remind you what it is by punching that smug look right off your fucking face. Now, get your lazy ass up, omega. When a better tells you to go fetch something, you move, and you do it right quick!"

Mac glanced up insolently at the delta, who was working himself up into a righteous fury because Mac wasn't moving, let alone cowering. Mac realized the delta felt Mac was disrespecting him by refusing to concede to his superiority in front of his friends, and it was pissing him off.

Not that Mac cared. Maybe he should have exercised a bit more discretion, but he'd had enough. It felt like he'd been walking on eggshells since he got back to the valley, and his resentment had been growing and swelling until he just couldn't hold back any longer.

He curled his lip and in his most insolent tone said, "Get your own fucking water. I'm not your slave."

That was it. It was *on*.

The delta roared and launched himself at Mac, but if he was expecting Mac not to fight back, he was sadly mistaken. Mac threw the delta off him fairly easily and got to his feet. Growing up, he'd learned to fight on the streets, down and dirty, but as soon as he'd achieved a measure of financial success, he'd paid to train as a boxer. He easily evaded the clumsy roundhouse punches the delta threw, and responded with carefully timed jabs that connected with the delta's chin and ribs.

They danced in a tight circle for several long moments. Although no one interfered, Mac could see the others out of the corners of his eyes, and none of them looked happy. They stood around, watching, and Mac was certain, waiting for Mac to go down.

He was almost sorry to disappoint them.

A solid punch to the delta's solar plexus put the delta down on the ground, gasping for air.

He scowled at the delta. "Fucker! Don't be foolish. Stay down."

The other workers finally moved, quickly surrounding and overpowering Mac. Although Mac struggled, he couldn't fight them all off at the same time. He went down under a flurry of fists and feet. Teeth snapped, tearing first the fabric of his shirt and pants, and then his flesh as a couple of men lost control and shifted. The beating seemed to go on forever, and when it stopped, Mac lay on the ground, bruised and bloodied, his breathing labored.

He barely noticed when he shifted. It was reflex; his wolf-self, although wounded, made a smaller target, and his sharp teeth and survival instinct would protect him better than his frailer man-skin could.

Through a thin red haze, a face hovered over him, and then felt himself lifted bodily from the ground. The pain was excruciating and he whined; gray crowded out the edge of his vision until he gratefully gave himself over to the darkness and knew no more.

* * *

WARM WETNESS DABBED GENTLY at his face, and he blinked awake, a low moan escaping his lips. He felt as if someone had fed him through the woodchipper, as if he'd been torn apart and nothing was holding the pieces of him together but pain.

"Shh. Lie still." The voice was low-pitched and somehow familiar. Mac frowned, trying to focus his eyes by sheer force of will. The blur he saw eventually coalesced into a handsome face with soft brown eyes and a gentle, friendly smile.

He knew that face, but it was a moment more before his brain fully came awake and he could put a name to it.

Blue Standish.

"You've taken a really bad beating, Mac, but thankfully, I got there before they could kill you. You have a few broken bones though. Your arm, a couple of fingers, and a few ribs. The doc says you may have a fractured jaw. He splinted your arm and your fingers, but couldn't do much for your ribs or jaw. Thank goodness we heal quickly."

Mac moaned again, but this time it wasn't from pain.

"Where are they? Those bastards jumped me because I beat one of them in a fair fight." Fuck! His jaw hurt when he talked, and he thought he might have a couple of loose teeth.

He quietly took stock of the rest of his body, moving each part slightly, and quickly agreed with Blue's assessment. His side hurt like a blue fuck when he tried to take a deep breath and his left arm was broken, as were at least two of the fingers on his right hand. He only hoped he'd broken them punching someone's face.

"They're long gone. I brought you to my cabin. You're safe here."

"I need to get home." He tried to rise and immediately regretted it. Every part of him screamed in protest of the movement. His eyes squeezed shut, fighting the tears of pain threatening to overflow.

Blue placed a gentle hand on his chest, urging him to stay still—not that he needed much urging. He hurt like a motherhumper. "You're not going anywhere. Look, we're not at my family's place. This is just a small cabin I keep near the logging camp. I've already sent word to your family that you're going to be here a while."

"Can't stay. Need to help my pa cut timber."

"Don't worry about that either. I sent a man down to the omega cabins to help him make his quota, and I also had additional rations brought to your ma. Your family's going to be fine, Mac. You need to concentrate on healing right now."

Mac groaned. Waves of pain washed over him with every movement. It'd been a far worse beating than he'd thought. He wouldn't be surprised if he had internal injuries. He was probably lucky to be alive.

"What were you thinking?"

He blinked up at Blue. "What?"

"You jumped a man for no reason. You know, that chip on

your shoulder is going to crush you someday if you don't find a way to get rid of it."

"What the fuck are you talking about?" A sharp pain in his jaw nearly took his breath away, and he had to fight the urge to cry out.

"Alvin and the others at the camp—the ones you fought with—said you attacked Alvin without reason. Out of the blue, just jumped him."

"That's bullshit! He ordered me to fetch water. I said no. Man, I am sick to death of people talking to me like I'm stupid or ordering me around like I'm a dog or a slave. I'm not any of those things."

"No one said you were stupid."

"Oh? Only a dog and a slave, huh?"

"See? There's that chip I was talking about." Blue glared at him. "Listen, you know how it is here. It's how we were all raised. I'm not saying that makes it right, but things aren't going to change just because you came back and say they should."

Mac growled and tried to sit up again. This time, he made it. He swung his legs over the side of the bunk, but his head swam and grayness threatened again. It took a few moments before he could fight through it and grew confident he wouldn't pass out. "I need to leave."

"Why? Because you don't like what I have to say? Listen, I'm responsible for you. I hired you, and you got hurt on my watch."

"I didn't just get hurt. I got jumped and beaten half to death by a bunch of men who think their shit doesn't stink just because they weren't born omegas."

Blue sighed, and the sound was heavy, as if weighted by guilt or regret or pure exasperation. Maybe it was all three. "Please, lie back, Mac. You can't go anywhere. You might be able to best an alpha when you're at a hundred percent, but I don't think you could beat down a half-lame rabbit in the condition you're in right now. Even if you could make it down the mountain on pure stubbornness, you won't live through another fight like the one you had. And believe me, the delta you beat down and his friends will be watching for you." He sighed again. "Don't make me force you to lie down, because I will if I have to."

Well, Blue had him there. He worried he couldn't even walk unaided, let alone fight his way past Blue and make it back to the settlement through a gauntlet of angry wolves. After a tense moment or two, he let Blue ease him down onto his back again.

"I'm going to take care of you. It's the least I can do. Like I said, the doc was here, and he left some herbal tea for you to take. Comfrey, I think he called it. Probably tastes like shit, but I also have willow tea to help with pain and a nice chicken broth ready for you after you drink it. He also said you should shift and stay in your wolf-skin whenever possible. You'll heal faster that way."

"Why are you doing this?"

Blue cocked his head at him. "I told you. I'm responsible for you."

"No, you're not."

"Yes, I am."

"No, you aren't."

Blue cracked a smile that lit up his eyes. "We can play this game all day, you know. I am responsible for you. This is what an alpha does. We protect."

"No, alphas hunt. They've always hunted. Nobody protected shit except for themselves."

Blue shook his head at him. "Is that what you think? That all we do is hunt? We protect the pack from outsiders. When one of the pack is injured, we take care of him and his family."

"Since when?"

"Since, well…since always."

"You must've been living with a different pack than the one I grew up in, then. No alpha I ever knew helped an omega when they were hurt."

"Then that's the alpha's failing. Look I know things weren't good when you left, and maybe they're not so great even now, but only because it's time for a change. Maybe we all need to take a look at what our pack is, and what it's supposed to be."

"What do you mean?"

Blue dipped the cloth he still held into a pan of water and dabbed at Mac's face again. Mac tried to push him away, but Blue refused to let him. "Stop." He patted a cut over Mac's eye. "I've been asking questions like these for a while now. Years, really. Things just… Well, they never sat right with me when they banished you. I really thought you were dead, Mac."

"Yeah, well, I thought so, too, for a while."

"I'll bet." Blue's smile was like a beam of sunshine breaking through the darkness, for all it was fleeting. A somber expression replaced it. "I owe you an apology. I knew you won that fight with Luc back when we were kids. I should've stood up for you. As an alpha, I should've protected you, but I was afraid."

Mac was stunned by Blue's admission. An alpha *never* apologized to an omega. He blinked and stammered. "Well, y-you were just a kid too. My banishment's not on you. It's on the pack elders."

"Yeah, well, I've still always felt guilty about it. That's when I started to really think about our pack structure. At first, I asked my family why things were the way they were, but they told me I was wrong to question things and flat-out refused to talk about it. I couldn't let it go though. I started looking for answers elsewhere."

He put the cloth back into the pan of water and stood up. Mac watched as he took a teakettle down from a shelf and ladled water into it. He put the teakettle on a woodstove to heat. "Eventually, I talked to Jasper Wynne. Do you remember him?"

Mac tried to think. "I think so, maybe. He was an omega, wasn't he? An old man, lived by himself, roughing it out in the woods beyond the settlement."

"That's right. Turns out, he was forced to the fringes of the pack because he liked to tell stories about the times when we still lived in the old country." He stood at a small rough-hewn kitchen table. After removing a pinch of some sort of leaf from a paper packet, he put it into a mortar, and began grinding it with a pestle. "According to Jasper, back in the old country every member of the pack was just as valued as all the others. We all had our jobs to do, but none of us were better or less than the others." Blue looked back at him. "I want to believe that. I really do." He put the herbs into a cup and placed the mortar and pestle to the side.

"But you don't."

The teakettle whistled. Blue lifted it and poured steaming water over the herbs in the mug. "I don't know. I've been confused a lot lately. I just don't know what or who to believe."

Mac closed his eyes. Just when he thought he might've made an ally... Why couldn't Blue see things for the way they were? Why did he continually vacillate between believing and not believing?

The answer came to him suddenly, like a beam of light cutting through thick storm clouds.

Blue didn't believe for the same reason no other alphas believed—or deltas or gammas or omegas for that matter.

They didn't understand because all they knew was the way things had always been in Wolf Valley. Anything else sounded too much like a fairy tale to be true.

He needed to change that. He needed to open their eyes, and there was only one way he could think of to do it.

"I promise I'll stay here and get well, let you tend me, but in return, I want your word on something. Your word as an alpha."

Blue cocked his head, looking both surprised and intrigued. "What do you want me to promise?"

"When I'm well enough to go home to my parents' cabin, I want you to go with me. I want you to come in and talk to them, see what it's like to live as an omega."

Blue blinked, a look of stunned surprise coloring his features. Then he hesitantly nodded. "All right. You have my word." His apprehension was clear, and his agreement, no matter how cautiously given, showed a certain amount of bravery Mac hadn't thought he'd possessed. Blue's worth inched up in Mac's eyes.

Mac couldn't help the small smile that tilted his lips before pain washed it away again. It was a long shot, but maybe, just maybe, he could sway Blue Standish to his way of thinking after all.

CHAPTER 5

The days passed quickly, far faster than Blue anticipated they would. He'd thought for sure each day would stretch out like an eternity, but he'd been happily mistaken. Two weeks had already flown by, but Blue found having Mac in the cabin wasn't a chore at all—it was fun. At least, it was after Mac promised to behave himself in exchange for Blue's pledge to live as an omega for a while.

It took a little doing, on both their parts though. It was harder than Blue would've thought for him to step away from the alpha mindset and stop issuing orders or assuming Mac didn't know what to do. He found out quickly that Mac's brain functioned just as well—or better—than his own. Mac wasn't only drop dead sexy—he was smart, quick to learn, and most surprisingly, under the gruff exterior, had a sense of humor.

As for himself, Blue was learning alphas often came across as condescending assholes. At least, that's what Mac told him he was being. Wolf-splaining, Mac called it when Blue felt the urge to explain how to do something to Mac.

I'm a grown-ass adult, Blue. Believe it or not, I can even tie my own fucking shoes without your directions.

Blue huffed a quiet laugh. Although he understood Mac's point, he had to wonder how Mac continued to walk upright under the weight of the gigantic chip on his shoulder. In the beginning, Blue felt as if he was walking on eggshells, trying to be sensitive, and careful of what he said to Mac. But it was so fucking hard. He believed it was in his nature to guide, and he'd always thought it was in Mac's to be guided. As it turned out, he was wrong. Big-time. Things finally came to a head about five days after Blue brought Mac to the cabin.

Mac started in with what Blue had already come to realize was Mac's favorite line. "I'm a grown-ass adult—"

Blue had reached the end of his patience. It'd been a trying day. There was a positive deluge going on outside, the hard rain turning the mountainside into a quagmire of mud. The roof of the cabin, which needed patching three years ago and which Blue had yet to do, began leaking again. He accidentally burned the eggs he'd scrambled for breakfast, and to top everything off, he had a whopper of a headache. He was done. Done! "I know, I know! You're an adult and you can tie your own fucking shoes. I get it. Really, I do. But you don't know everything, Mac, and if you think you do, then you're a narcissist. I absolutely refuse to second-guess everything I say to you in fear you're going to explode again! Cut me a freaking break, will you? I've done nothing but try to help you."

He was upset and angry and had worked himself up into such a state that he was mortified to feel tears burn the corners of his eyes. He frantically tried to blink them away before they fell.

"Whoa." Mac took a step toward him. "Hey, don't do that. There's no reason to get so upset. I'm sorry."

A low growl rumbled in Blue's chest. "I don't need your pity."

To Blue's shock, Mac chuckled. "Good, because you don't have it. What you *do* have is my gratitude. There. I said it. I'm grateful. I really am. Blue, I know you didn't have to take me in after the fight. You could've just let them kill me or sent me back to the omega cabins or just left me there to bleed in the dirt. Maybe you should've. I know you're going to take twelve kinds of shit from your family and the other alphas when they find out you've been taking care of me."

Blue lifted a shoulder. "Like I care what the other alphas think."

"Well, maybe not, but you *do* care what your family thinks, and Argyle and Enoch are going to turn purple when they find out."

Blue shrugged again, but he knew Mac was right. He was going to catch right and proper hell when word got back to his folks that he'd taken a Fuller, the lowest of all omegas, to his cabin. Still, he stood by his decision. "It was the right thing to do. It's what alphas are *supposed* to do."

"Alphas aren't always concerned with doing the right thing, unless it's the right thing for *them.*"

"Not all of us, Mac. That's what I'm trying to show you. Some of us care. I'm not saying we're perfect or that it's right for the rest to be the assholes they are, but we're not all like Luc and his buddies."

Mac looked away, and his cheeks pinked. "I guess maybe I'm starting to realize that. It's just this whole caste thing the pack insists on keeping is so barbaric, I'm having trouble accepting it. I don't want to accept it, actually. I won't."

The tension in Blue melted away, and he was hit with the urge to lighten the mood. "Between you and me, I'm not saying you're wrong. I wonder about it myself sometimes. I mean, is it right to keep doing something that feels wrong just because that's the way it's always been?"

Mac gaped at him as if he'd just grown an elephant's trunk and zebra stripes. "Wow. I never thought I'd hear those words from an alpha's lips."

Blue snorted, even though he could feel his cheeks heating. "And if you tell anyone, I'll deny it to my last breath. So, tell me about being an omega. How are we going to do this?"

In truth, Blue didn't know how Mac's plan would work—everyone in Wolf Valley knew Blue. He'd lived here all his life, and besides, the omegas would be able to smell the alpha on him.

But Mac insisted he had a plan, so Blue went along with it. After all, if it didn't work, no one would be worse for the wear, right? And if it did, well, maybe Blue would finally have answers to the questions that'd plagued him for so long.

"The omegas will go along because they'll all be curious to see how an alpha will cope with working like an omega. None of the alphas will even notice. They never notice omegas unless they want something. Plus, you can wear a disguise. A gimme cap. That and keeping your head down will hide your face from anyone who happens to glance our way."

Since there was nothing untrue in what Mac said, Blue simply nodded. It was true, after all. The omegas would be curious—as would he—but they'd be beneath the other alphas notice. If he kept his head down, nobody would know he was there.

He pushed his worries aside. It would be fine. He wouldn't be doing anything wrong, per se. There was no pack law against an alpha working with omegas—alphas could do whatever they wanted. It's just that no other alpha would consider doing menial labor, particularly in the company of omegas.

Anyway, it wouldn't happen for a while yet. For now, Blue was happy taking care of Mac. It pacified his alpha wolf-self's need to protect, he supposed. And, he admitted, he was growing to like Mac, maybe more than was good for him.

Mac was healing nicely. The colorful bruises were beginning to fade, and the cuts scabbed over without any sign of infection. The broken arm and fingers would take a bit longer to heal, of course, but Mac said they pained him less than they had, and being in wolf-form aided the healing process. Although his broken arm was set with a birch bark cast, his injured fingers were only taped together for support. Blue continued to feed Mac the comfrey tea, too, even though Mac complained without fail every time Blue presented him with the cup.

"It tastes like shit!" Mac wrinkled his nose and glared at the cup as if willing it to burst into flame. "If I want to taste dirt, I can lick the forest floor."

"Medicine rarely tastes good. Stop being such a puppy and drink it." Blue bit back a smile even as he tried to sound stern. Mac was adorable when he pouted about taking the tea.

Eventually, after much grumbling and complaining, Mac would drain the cup. Blue always found his pained expression at the tea's taste hysterical, and would chuckle. Then Mac would push the cup away with his good arm and glower at him. It was practically a ritual with them.

"If you're done laughing at my misfortune, I'm hungry. What's for dinner?"

Blue surged into outright laughter as he cleared away the teacup. "Can't hurt too bad if you're thinking with your stomach. Beans with ham hocks and collard greens."

Mac offered a small smile. "My ma calls that 'leather britches.'"

He nodded. "Mine too. Everybody 'round here calls it

that, I reckon. Got us some of my ma's apple stack cake for dessert." The glow of anticipation he saw warm Mac's smile made it worth Blue asking his ma to bake it. He'd gone down the mountain early that morning while Mac was still asleep to fetch it—dodging questions from his mother about what he was doing up at the shack and when he was coming home.

Blue could cook well enough to survive—he was a fair hand at making beans and ham hocks—but baking wasn't in his wheelhouse, and he wanted something sweet. It was women's work, his father said, which is why the men folk in the family never learned how, but Blue believed you had to have a talent for baking, and it was one gift he freely admitted he didn't possess. He was happy enough to let his ma do all the baking for him.

He served up dinner, and they ate in companionable silence, both seemingly intent on enjoying the meal. Only when they'd scraped the last bits of apple stack cake from their plates and finished their coffee did their conversation resume. When it did, it was regarding the last subject on earth Blue would've suspected.

"I see you looking at me sometimes."

Blue blinked at Mac, surprised, then stared down at his cup. As if suddenly realizing his cup was empty and if he didn't fill it, the world as he knew it just might end, he jumped up and sprinted to the stove for the large battered tin coffeepot. He carried it back and refilled both their cups, hoping that Mac would change the subject before Blue was forced to comment one way or the other.

Mac didn't. He just stared at Blue, the silence stretching between them, growing uncomfortable.

Blue didn't know what to say. The truth? Or a lie that might spare his dignity? "Boy, that apple stack cake sure was good, huh?"

"It was great. But what I said was, I see you looking at me sometimes."

Blue refused to meet Mac's eyes. He couldn't, not if he wanted to keep his jangling nerves under control. His hand shook as he poured a little cream into his coffee. "I know. I heard you. Of course, I look at you. Can't help it, can I? You're right here in my cabin. Nothing else to look at except the same four walls."

"That's not what I meant, and I think you know it."

"What *did* you mean, then?" He kept his gaze on his cup, sipped his coffee, and burned his tongue.

"You like me, right?"

Blue shrugged, still refusing to meet Mac's gaze. "You're okay. For an omega, I mean."

Mac chuckled. "Now you're just trying to piss me off because you don't want to answer the question. Come on. I've been out in the world, Blue. I know when a man is interested in me."

Blue felt his cheeks catch fire. His hand shook so much coffee slopped over the rim of his cup and splashed on the table. "Shit!" He shook the hot coffee from his hand, grabbed a dishcloth, and mopped up the mess.

"You know, you're kind of cute when you're nervous. For an alpha, I mean."

In absence of a snappy comeback, Blue settled for denial. "I don't know what you're talking about."

"Yes, you do. Stop lying."

Blue made the mistake of finally locking gazes with Mac. Those bright blue eyes held him, pinned him in place as sure as if Mac had nailed Blue's feet to the floor and refused to let him look away again. It searing right through his skin into his soul, and he knew he couldn't lie. "Yeah. I think you're sex on a stick. Okay? Happy? I have since we were kids."

Mac sat back in his chair, his grin both smug and sly. "See? That wasn't so hard, was it?"

"Actually, it is hard. Rock hard." He shifted slightly in his seat, although he kept watching Mac, anxious to see if he could wipe the self-satisfied smile off Mac's face with a cold dose of embarrassment. Turns out, he couldn't.

Mac, it seemed, didn't embarrass easily.

"Good. That's just the way I like 'em. Hard."

Okay, he hadn't quite seen that one coming. Mac was into men? Why hadn't Blue noticed in the last two weeks? Maybe Mac just wasn't into *him*. That could explain why Mac hadn't shown any interest, even when Blue sponged him down or helped him change clothes.

His cheeks burned as humiliation flooded him. Rejected by an omega! It didn't get any worse than that, did it? His only consolation was no one would ever learn about it. "Yeah, well, don't worry. I'm not going to try to jump you if that's what you're thinking."

"Why not? Too good to have an omega suck your dick?"

Blue dropped his metal coffee cup on the table. The rest of his coffee splashed out, and it rolled off the edge, falling to the floor with a loud *clang*. It bounced once, and Blue had to chase it down. He picked it up and carried it to the wash-basin, then rinsed it off as an excuse not to look at Mac. "That's not a subject we talk openly about around here. A man could get banished for having such thoughts."

"For fuck's sake, why? What's it anyone's business who they bring to their bed?"

Sighing, Blue dried his hands on another dishtowel and turned to face Mac. He held up two fingers. "Two reasons. First, men don't fuck other men. Not out in the open, not around here. Secondly, maybe even more importantly, alphas don't bed omegas. Come on, Mac. You know that. It's just not done."

Mac sprang out of the chair, and it clattered over on its side. He stalked across the cabin toward Blue. "You know, I'm sick to death hearing about how alphas don't do this, and omegas can't do that. I've a good mind to break all the rules, right here, right now." He stopped mere inches away from Blue.

"How are you going to do that?" Blue took an inadvertent step backward—Mac was standing so close Blue could feel his body heat.

"Like this."

In the next moment, Blue was in Mac's arms, being kissed hard, a soft wet tongue delving into his mouth, sliding across his own. Strong hands clutched his back, fingers digging into his flesh. A hard cock pressed against his thigh, while his own thickened in response. When Mac finally broke the kiss, Blue was left breathless.

"Holy shit."

Mac watched him carefully, as if studying him. "Well? Tell me you're not pissed at me."

"No. Not angry. I'm…horny as fuck though." Blue snorted a short laugh.

"Oh, see, now that I can work with." Mac grinned at him and began trying to shrug out of his shirt, a little awkwardly because of the cast on his arm and his taped fingers. "Give me a hand. We have too many clothes on."

Blue shook his head. "Mac, somebody might come. What if my mother or father or one of my brothers walks in?"

Mac sighed. "For an alpha, you're being a chickenshit. Okay, stick a chair under the doorknob if you're nervous. Tape paper over the windows. I don't give a fuck. We both want this, and you know it. We're two grown men, and I'll be fucked sideways if I'm going to let the stupid rules of this pack keep us from having what we both want. Shit, what we *need.*"

67

KIERNAN KELLY

Blue curled his lips in an answering smile. He hurried to drag a chair to the door and tilted it, wedging it under the knob, then cast a look at the window, making sure the curtains were drawn, silently blessing his ma for sewing them up for him. As he turned back to Mac, he stripped his shirt off and tossed it to the floor.

Shyness made him look down and bite his lip as he walked toward Mac. He was unused to the feeling—alphas weren't shy by nature—but he'd never been so boldly propositioned before, nor had he ever been so keenly attracted to another man. The few times he'd indulged himself had been with humans in the dark, filthy alley behind the only gay bar he knew of, and then only during the exceedingly rare trips he'd made to the city by himself.

Everything about Mac turned Blue on, from Mac's handsome face to his lean, hard body. Even Mac's acerbic wit made Blue's body sit up and take notice. Right now, his cock was hard, pressing against his fly as if straining for release.

Mac was struggling to take off his shirt. He'd managed to get it over his head, but then it got stuck on his cast. Blue hurried to help and eased the fabric off.

Mac's chest was wide and smooth except for a thin trail of hair tracking down the middle and continuing in a straight line over his stomach. It disappeared beneath his pant waistband. Blue wanted to lick it, to drag his tongue over that tempting trail until he found the treasure hidden under the worn denim.

Then he realized there was nothing keeping him from following his impulses. He grinned, then began kissing and nibbling along Mac's jaw, unhurriedly making his way over Mac's throat, chest, and stomach, until he reached the zippered fly.

"Use your teeth, alpha."

The stern order stopped him in his tracks, but instead of

being upset or angry at the authoritative tone in Mac's voice, Blue found it turned him on even more. His body burned anew with need, his balls swelling under the now-uncomfortably tight crotch of his pants. He quickly divested himself of his jeans and shucked his underwear while he was at it. His cock sprang free, and he sighed as the cool air hit his hot flesh.

"Did you hear me?"

Blue nodded and then guided Mac toward the bed, walking him backward. After he helped Mac lie back, he bent over Mac's crotch. Mac's cock was clearly outlined under the soft denim, and it looked to be a beauty. Blue carefully worked the top button free. He threw a teasing look up at Mac, then opened his mouth and blew out a hot breath over the bulge under the fly. His reward was the sound of Mac sucking in air between his teeth, and hips arching to meet his lips.

He continued to blow air over Mac's dick, until Mac writhed beneath him. "Stop fucking teasing me!"

Blue chuckled, then reluctantly gave in and returned to the zipper. Taking it between his teeth, he haltingly worked it open, revealing what he'd discovered since bringing Mac to his cabin. Before, he'd thought it hot and sexy, but now he added convenient to the list.

Mac did not wear underwear.

His cock, thick and rosy red, sprang free through the open fly and bumped against Blue's cheek. The smell of man, the scent of musk, warmth, and sweat, reached Blue's nose, and he breathed it all the way in. Lifting his head, he studied Mac's cock.

Blue had been right—it *was* a beauty. Perfectly shaped with a thick stalk and smooth, fat head, it was framed by a nearly perfect triangle of black hair. Mac's balls were still tucked inside his jeans, but that was one problem Blue was quick to solve. He forced himself away from Mac's dick and yanked Mac's pants off the rest of the way.

Mac's large balls were swollen and covered in dark hair. Blue gave in to temptation and tongued them, then sucked one into his mouth.

"Fuck, Blue! Aw, fuck."

In time, Blue thought. *Right now, I just want to suck you.* He played with Mac's balls for a while, then finally moved on to his cock.

Mac's taste was earthy, as ancient as their bloodline, and it drew a hungry response from the depths of Blue's core. He took Mac in deep, sucking hard.

From the corner of his eye, he saw Mac's fingers twisting in the sheets. "Shit! I'm going to come, Blue."

No, no. He wanted to see Mac come, wanted to know what Mac's face looked like at that moment when time stopped and the world ceased to have meaning except for the bolt of pleasure spearing through him. He let go and eased himself up onto Mac's hips, letting their cocks rub together.

Taking both of their dicks in his hand, he stroked them together, faster and faster, harder, until his own climax swelled up and crashed over him just as Mac came. Their semen spurted in twin arcs over Mac's belly as Blue stroked them both to completion.

"Fuck. Just...fuck." Mac was breathing hard, as if he'd run a mile. "That was so good, Blue. God, your mouth is so fucking hot."

"You taste good." Blue smiled, feeling weary but very, very satisfied. He rolled off Mac and stretched out next to him. "We'll last longer next time, yeah?" He bit his lip and frowned. "There *is* going to be a next time, right?"

"Oh, yeah. Fuck yeah. Gonna go all night." Mac grinned. He traced a finger through the come coating his belly. "Feels like I was storing it up for winter."

Blue barked a laugh, then sobered. "Your arm okay? Your fingers? I didn't hurt you, did I?"

"Yeah, they're good. The rest of me is even better."

Blue laughed and then yawned. Was he this tired before they'd gotten naked? He didn't know and cared less. His eyes drifted shut, and the last conscious thought he had before drifting off to sleep was that the chair was still blocking the door.

Then again, since he and Mac were both naked and lying next to each other on the bed, it was probably safer that way.

CHAPTER 6

"Nobody is going to know. You reek of my scent. They'll just think you're another omega." Mac pulled the brim of his ball cap lower over Blue's eyes and stood back, eyeing him with a critical gaze. "You look like an omega. You smell like an omega. Trust me. Nobody will question you. Just keep your head down, keep away from anyone who's not an omega, and follow me, okay?"

"I hope you're right. I don't want to have to explain why an alpha is trying to impersonate an omega to anybody."

"We talked about this. The only way you'll ever really learn what it's like to be an omega in Wolf Valley is to live like one for a while."

"I know. I just don't want to have to explain it to anyone else."

"Keep your mouth shut and your head down, and you won't have to." Mac began walking, trusting Blue to stay behind him. He pushed through brush, following a deer trail from Blue's cabin. He skirted the logging camp and farther all the way down to the valley. It'd been full dark when they set out, both carrying axes propped against their shoulders—

by the time they reached the omega cabins, the sun was rising.

A steady stream of omega men followed the road up the side of the mountain to the area where timber could be cut for the pack's use. Mac and Blue merged into the line, following the last couple of men up.

Mac's arm had healed well and barely pained him at all anymore. Blue had done an excellent job at playing nursemaid. He smirked, thinking nursing wasn't the only thing Blue was good at. Blue could work a cock like nobody's business too. Sucking dick sure had made the six weeks he'd spent in Blue's cabin a lot more tolerable than it would've been otherwise.

He'd stayed and let Blue take care of him without arguing —much—keeping his part of the bargain they'd made. Now it was Blue's turn. For the next month or so, he was determined Blue would live the life of an omega. They'd work at omega chores and sleep out in a tent with the other omegas unfortunate enough not to have a permanent cabin. With winter breathing down their necks, it would be uncomfortable at best. It would give Blue a raw look at how hard the life of an omega could be.

The first chore was to cut timber for the camp's use. They'd be out every day cutting trees and splitting logs, stockpiling cords for the coming winter. It was backbreaking work as Blue was soon to find out.

They took up spots on the splitting teams and spent the next four hours at it, hacking fallen tree trunks into more manageable pieces, then dragging them off on sledges to where other men split the logs into cordwood. By the time their shift was over, Blue's hands were a blistered, bleeding mess.

Mac went to his parents' cabin and returned shortly with a piece of clean, if well-used cloth. He tore it into smaller strips and used it to bandage Blue's hands. "Don't worry. Your hands will callus soon enough."

"Is the work always this hard? My back is fucking killing me."

"You get used to it after a while. Don't forget, these men have been doing this since they came of age. Come on. Time to get into the forest."

"The forest? What for?"

"Hey, those apples aren't going to pick themselves. And the last of the late berries are ripe. Plus, I think there's a patch of wild carrot near the blackberry bushes, and I promised ma I'd try to find some ramps."

Blue wrinkled his nose at the mention of the wild onions. "I thought the gammas took care of the food."

"They cook it, sure. But who do you think needs to pick it? The gammas won't dirty their hands gathering produce."

Blue hissed as Mac finished tying the last strip of cloth. "Damn, that hurts. How the hell am I supposed to wield an ax again tomorrow?"

"You won't. Tomorrow we've got hunting to do."

Shaking his head, Blue looked at him as if he'd lost his mind. "Omegas can't hunt, Mac. You know that."

"Did I say we were going to hunt for meat?" He lowered his voice to a whisper. "Tomorrow starts ginseng season, doesn't it?"

Blue's eyes flashed open wide. "What do you know about ginseng?"

Mac blew a soft raspberry. "Everybody who grew up on this mountain knows about it. I know enough to know it's worth its weight in gold."

"It is, but it's forbidden for anyone to harvest it."

"Who made up that stupid rule?"

Blue shrugged. "I don't know. It's just always been that way. The ginseng grows up on the mountainside. On feder-

74

ally protected land, human law says harvesting wild ginseng is illegal."

"Well, horseshit on that. Not all the land around here is government owned. We're going to go look for some, and if we find it on pack land, we're going to pick it. Take it down to the city and sell it to the humans and use the money to help the omegas this winter."

"But it's forbidden!"

Mac hissed and glanced around. "Keep your voice down! Did you ever ask yourself why it's forbidden? It's another one of those stupid pack rules that make no sense, but nobody ever dares to challenge them. Listen, if there's one thing you need to learn about omegas, it's that not all of us survive the cold season. Look around you, Blue. You see these people? Most them you're looking at don't have warm cabins to go to after work. They set up camp just like we are and sleep in tents. Right now, it's not bad. Our body heat will be enough to keep the tent warm, but imagine doing this in three feet of snow with a blizzard blowing."

"Why don't some of the omega families take them in?"

Mac grunted. "They do, but there's just not enough room for everyone. Besides, that's not the point. It's still a fucked up way to live. My family used to be the lowest of the low -- you remember, right?"

Blue bit his lip, but nodded.

"It was years before my pa could rate a cabin, and then it was the worst one in the community. The one they still live in, mind you. These poor people haven't been as lucky."

"I'm sorry, Mac." Blue looked miserable. "But, ginseng—"

"Do you trust me?"

"What?"

"I asked if you trust me."

Blue gave a slow nod. "Sure. Yeah, I trust you, Mac."

"Good. Then tomorrow, we hunt for ginseng. Right now,

we need to grab baskets and head out to that stand of apple trees on the north side before they're picked clean."

* * *

THEY FOUND a place where a huge tree had uprooted and spent the night in a tent pitched in the lee of the exposed roots. Mac was right—their body heat kept the small space warm enough, but that would only last until the winter winds really began to blow. When the temperatures dropped below freezing, their survival would depend on heavy furs and blankets, and the only way for omegas to get them was at the discretion of the alphas.

Mac was determined to change that, and ginseng was the answer.

The idea to hunt ginseng came to him while he was laid up at Blue's cabin. He'd never even thought about it before, not until the last couple of years. At a gallery opening, he'd met a human man who'd written a book on the subject. Turns out, ginseng grew wild in Appalachia, was avidly gathered on private land from the first of September through the first of December, and brought an absurdly high price from buyers.

Wolf Valley was well hidden from humans. If there was ginseng on the mountain, no one would be out trying to gather it except Blue and Mac, especially since picking it was taboo among the pack. One of the reasons, he knew, was because while the pack considered the entire mountain to be theirs, in reality, it wasn't. Only the land the community sat on, and the few acres they harvested timber from belonged to them. The rest was government land, and it was illegal to gather ginseng on federally owned land.

The mystery lay in the fact that the pack usually didn't give two wet shits about human law. Plus, to his knowledge, one even bothered to hunt for ginseng growing on land that legally belonged to the pack. The reason why ginseng was off limits escaped him.

In the end, he found he really didn't care anyway. Legally harvested ginseng would go a long way to solving a lot of problems for the omegas of the pack, rules be damned.

He could just go down to the city and hit the bank, withdraw a bunch of his own money and give it to the omegas—which he would do if his plan didn't work out—but that would only solve the problem for this season. He wanted to give the omegas a more permanent solution.

If he could harvest enough ginseng, he could use it to seed a crop. The omegas could farm it and earn a decent living from it without having to risk the human authorities. That, at least, was the plan.

The sun found them dressed and ready to go. Mac and Blue ate a quick breakfast of biscuits and gravy cooked over a campfire, along with cups of boiling hot coffee. It didn't take long to wash the few implements and break camp. By the time they were done, only the warm ashes of their campfire showed anyone had passed the night there.

They headed up the west side of the mountain, in the opposite direction of the logging camp and the omega timber-cutting crews. There were a couple of pack-owned acres on that side of the mountain, and they were least likely to be discovered picking ginseng there—if they found any.

When he peeked under the bandages, Blue's hands looked like chopped meat, and Mac was glad he didn't need to watch Blue suffer trying to swing an ax again today. Their tents, clothes, and utensils were packed into their backpacks, and all they carried were a few empty burlap bags.

Blue nearly tripped over an exposed root and cursed under his breath. "How do you even know what ginseng looks like?"

"I met a man once who wrote a book about it. He said there are these things called 'companion plants.' Black cohosh and goldenseal are two of them."

Blue tossed him a dubious look. "Well, that's convenient."

Mac shrugged. "What can I say? As a photographer, I've met lots of interesting people over the years. I also know how to throw a vase on a pottery wheel, and that lobster bisque soup is made using lobster shells. That knowledge, however, doesn't apply here. The bit about the ginseng does."

"Okay, okay. So you were saying goldenseal? Those plants with the little white flowers?"

"Yup. Those are the ones. He also said ginseng likes to grow in deep, dark soil, with lots of leaf litter."

Blue laughed. "Yeah, well, that narrows it down. Not. You just described the entire mountain."

"Go ahead and laugh." Mac tried to sound stern, but a smile escaped him. "Anyway, the man said a mature ginseng plant is hard to spot, but it'll have clusters of little greenish white flowers and red berries."

"Red berries... Hey! I think I've seen those plants!" Blue sounded excited. "Sure! I think there's some growing near the mouth of the stream."

Mac's smile grew into a grin. "Well, what are we waiting for? Let's go!"

Blue took the lead, and Mac followed close on his heels. They hiked up the mountainside, eventually meeting up with Jewel Creek. Here it was only a skinny watercourse, barely more than a trickle, snaking through thick underbrush. Eventually, Mac spotted the thin, tumbling waterfall that marked Jewel Creek's beginning.

"Okay, do you remember where you might've seen the ginseng?"

Blue nodded and began scanning the ground. "There! See the berries?"

Mac had to look hard before he found what Blue was pointing at. Scattered across the root system of a stand of hickory, nearly invisible, were several small plants bearing greenish-white flowers and clusters of bright red berries.

Ginseng.

Mac hooted with excitement and bent down. He carefully extracted the plants, taking care not to damage the roots. He held one of the thick, vaguely carrot-shaped white roots up to the light. "Not much to look at, huh? But it'll bring a king's ransom down in the city."

Blue grinned at him and looked for another plant to harvest. He laughed out loud when he found one and gave Mac the thumbs-up sign.

They spent the day combing the hillside for ginseng plants. By the time the sun started setting, they'd filled two sacks, had aching backs from bending over, and were covered in dirt and bits of old leaves.

"I need a shower, Mac." Blue bent backward, rubbing the small of his back as if to work out kinks. "I smell like the wrong side of a wild boar."

"Sorry. Omegas don't have the luxury of indoor plumbing. We'd have to haul in water, heat it, and empty it into a tub to wash, and that's only if we had a cabin, which we don't."

Blue looked aghast. "So where are we supposed to wash?"

"Jewel Creek. We wash downstream from the settlement."

"Are you crazy? That water is freezing already!"

Mac hefted his sack to his shoulder. "Better get used to it, or you're going to get mighty stinky over the next few weeks." He began to retrace their steps toward the settlement. "Come on now. Let's hustle. We need to clean these roots and get some sleep. Tomorrow we need to do our chores. We don't want to tip anyone off that we're up to something."

"Yeah, you know if we get caught, we'll be in big trouble, Mac. But what about picking more ginseng?" He held up his bag. "Do you think this enough?"

"I don't know. Depends on how much we can sell it for. We'll hunt tomorrow afternoon and every spare minute we get until the first snows. Then we'll take them down to the city and find a buyer. Plus, I want enough to lay aside to replant." He quickly outlined his plan to have the omegas farm ginseng.

"Mac, I hate to tell you this, but the alphas won't allow it. It's against pack rules, remember?"

"Do you think the alphas know everything? The omegas keep secrets, Blue. They have to, in order to survive. We'll take as many into our cabins as we can to keep them freezing in winter, although we can't fit everyone, even though the alphas say we're not to share our cabins. We give food to those who need more than they're allotted. Our womenfolk are practiced healers, even though pack law forbids us the knowledge of healing plants. This will just be another secret we have to keep."

Blue looked stunned, and it was all Mac could do not to laugh. "I… I had no idea."

"I know you didn't. That's why you're here. To learn, and maybe help change things."

CHAPTER 7

By the time the first fat flakes of snow drifted down from a gunmetal gray sky, Blue was well and truly done with pretending to be an omega.

He was always tired, never feeling like he'd gotten enough sleep. He was usually hungry, because their rations were smaller than he was used to eating. His back always hurt from chopping and hauling wood, although his hands no longer blistered from swinging an ax. And he stank.

The water in the stream was freezing cold, and he couldn't wash very well with the little water they could heat up in a pot on the campfire.

Most of all, he was sick and tired of the way people treated him.

People he'd known his entire life looked at him with derision, as if he was dirt under their feet, and that was only when they deigned to notice him at all. No one knew it was Blue, of course. At first, he just kept the brim of his hat pulled low and stayed in the shadows, but as the weather cooled, he took to wearing a hooded jacket, with a scarf pulled over the lower half of his face. No one recognized him, but he thought it might be partly because no one bothered to look very closely at any of the omegas.

He was shouted at, ordered around, and generally treated like a slave by the alphas, and not much better by the deltas and the gammas. Blue felt guilty—he just hadn't realized what it was like for the omegas. Why did people treat them this way? Even more importantly, why did they continue to put up with it?

These were questions he'd put to Mac the night before as they'd sat at the campfire, relaxing a while before going to bed.

"Like you said yourself, it's the way things have always been." Mac was cleaning his nails with a small knife. "It's pack law."

"But it's not right!"

Mac smiled at him. "That's good to hear, Blue."

"It's good to hear that nothing is right in the pack?"

"No, but it's good to hear you say it." Mac put his knife away and looked around as if to make sure no one was watching, then leaned in and stole a hot, wet kiss. "You didn't think that way before."

Blue smiled and gave a little shrug. "I questioned things before, but I never really understood what you and the other omegas went through."

"The gammas and deltas, too, although they don't have it as rough as the omegas. The only ones in the pack who have life easy are the alphas."

They sat in silence for a while, each lost in his own thoughts. Blue poked at the fire with a stick and watched bright embers float up into the darkness.

"Blue? What do you supposed happened to make things the way they are? Are all packs like this?"

"Remember the old man I told you about? Jeb Latham, the one who used to tell stories about our people when they lived in the old country? He said once upon a time all of us were valued the same. Each did our part, and everyone shared equally in the rewards. But once we settled in Wolf Valley, things started to change. Some of us decided we were stronger and therefore *better* than everyone else."

"The alphas?"

Blue felt his cheeks heat up, embarrassed. "Yeah. I always wanted to believe we were the protectors of the pack, but now I realize that's not true. We take advantage of everyone, Mac. Someone needs to protect the pack from *us*."

Mac put a warm hand on his thigh. "Not from you. You're one of the good ones, Blue. You care, and you learned what it's like. You can change things."

Blue nodded. "Starting as soon as we get back from selling the ginseng, I swear it."

Mac reached for another kiss. "Tomorrow then?"

"Tomorrow."

An early morning storm was brewing as they hiked down the mountain carrying their sacks of ginseng roots slung over their shoulders. Snow came down harder, lazily coloring them and the forest white. By the time they reached the outskirts of the city, they resembled a pair of young Kris Kringles hauling sacks of toys.

Blue nudged Mac. "Have any idea how to find someone who wants to buy these roots?"

"Actually, yeah, I do. We're going to go ask inside that bar." He pointed his chin toward a small, slightly seedy-looking bar on the corner.

Blue frowned. "Um, no. We don't go into human bars. It's forbidden."

Mac growled at him. "If I hear you say something is forbidden one more time, I'm going to haul off and slam you with this sack."

He grinned sheepishly and nodded. "I can't help it. It's habit."

"Well, try. Let's go." Mac led the way through brush. They entered town on a street that terminated at the tree line. A corner bar called the Dew Drop Inn, according the small sign hanging over the door, was at the far end. Flickering in the window was a neon sign in the shape of a martini glass. Mac strode right up to the building and opened the door, ushering Blue inside.

It was dark inside the bar, and it took Blue's eyes a minute to adjust. There were a few tables and chairs set to one side and a long wooden bar running along the other. At the back of the room was a billiard table.

The only person in the place was the bartender, who looked up from where he stood, wiping down the bar with a rag. "We don't open until noon, fellas."

"Sorry. We just wanted to ask a question." Mac strode up to the bar. "Would you happen to know anyone who's in the market for fresh ginseng?"

The bartender arched an eyebrow. "You got some?"

"Yeah." Mac hefted his sack.

A low whistle met the sight of the heavy bag. "Looks like you got maybe fifty pounds of it. That's worth a pretty penny."

Mac nodded. "Know anybody?"

A cagey expression colored the bartender's face, and he shrugged. "Maybe, maybe not. You pick that on government land? That's illegal. Anyhow, I forget the guy's name."

Rolling his eyes, Mac set the sack down and dug into his pocket. He pulled out a bill and slid it over the bar. "Do you remember his name now?"

Blue's eyes widened. "That's a fifty! Mac, where'd you get that?"

Mac elbowed him. He lifted his chin toward the bartender. "So, do you remember?"

The bartender took the bill and shoved it into the pocket of the apron he wore. "His name is Mooney. Justice Mooney. He's one of the biggest buyers in the area. You'll find him over on Kearny Avenue. He rents out a storefront during ginseng season."

"And how do we get to Kearny Avenue from here?"

"Left at the light onto Sand Mine Road. It intersects with Kearny about four or five blocks in."

Mac lifted his sack again and nodded to the bartender. "Much obliged."

Blue smirked at the sarcasm heavy in Mac's voice as he followed him out the door of the bar. "Where did you get that money, Mac?"

"I brought it with me when I came home." Mac hurried along the sidewalk. "It was only a fifty, for God's sake. You sound like it was a million."

"Might as well be. Cash money is hard to come by at home."

Mac grunted. "We need to hurry if we're going to sell this and get back home before dark."

It seemed that was all he had to say on the subject of the fifty-dollar bill, but his misdirection only served to make Blue wonder what Mac *wasn't* telling him.

He pondered on it as they made their way to Kearny Avenue. The snow was falling heavier, and he knew it would be thicker yet up on the mountain. He shivered, thinking about the puny, cold tent they had waiting for them. "Mac, I sure would like to sleep in a real bed tonight. It's going to be awful cold up on the mountain."

Mac sighed. "I suppose it's time. You learned what it's like to be an omega, and that was the whole point, right? I can go back to my parents' cabin."

Blue stopped in his tracks. "What? No, that's not what I meant. I thought you'd be coming back to my cabin with me."

"Now, how do you suppose that would look to the pack, Blue? It was okay when I was convalescing, but now that I'm healed, it would look awful suspicious for two men to shack up together, wouldn't it?"

"I guess, maybe, but…"

Mac put up his hand. "Hold that thought. We're here." He pointed to a hand-lettered sign in the soaped-over window of a shop. "Buying ginseng. Top dollar."

A small bell jingled when he opened the door, and Mac preceded Blue into the store. It was warm inside, and a welcome relief to be out of the wind and cold. Blue pushed his hood back, appreciating the heat.

"Help you fellas?" A man sat behind a desk. He was bald and very round, his immense belly straining at the buttons on his shirt. A roll of fat encircled his throat, cushioning his chin and jowls. His eyes were small and blue, blinking behind a pair of round eyeglasses.

A scale sat on one side of his desk and a cash register on the other. His hands were folded between them, his sausage-like fingers interlaced. A plate holding a half-eaten sandwich was in front of him, and a .45 was within easy reach. Blue had no doubt the man would use the gun to protect his money and his ginseng if necessary. Maybe even his sandwich.

"Are you Justice Mooney?"

"The one and only."

Mac nodded. "Good. Got some ginseng to sell you."

"Well, let's take a look. Mind, you boys, I only buy quality goods."

"This is the best, I guarantee it." Mac hefted his bag onto the desk and opened it. He withdrew a plant and handed it to Mooney.

Mooney examined the plant with what looked to be a critical eye. "Very nice. How much you boys got?"

"I figure we got about fifty pounds between us."

Mooney motioned to the scale. "Let's weigh it, see what we're looking at."

Mac carefully extracted the ginseng from his and Blue's bags and weigh it. It came in at just over sixty-two pounds total.

Mooney took out a calculator and pressed a few buttons. "I pay two hundred a pound. That comes to—"

"Hmph." Mac huffed and began loading the ginseng back into the bags. "Thanks for your time."

"Wait! What are you doing?"

"We don't appreciate being taken advantage of, Mr. Mooney. Two hundred a pound is shit for quality ginseng like this, and you know it."

"All right, all right. Three hundred a pound."

"Six."

"That's outrageous! Four. And that's my final offer."

"Five."

Mooney's forehead creased in a scowl. "Four and half, and not a penny more."

"Sold."

They walked out of there lighter by sixty-two pounds and heavier by over twenty-seven thousand dollars. The money was in large bills, rubber banded and stuffed into large, fat envelopes.

Blue grinned. "I thought Mooney was going to have a heart attack when you told him he had to pay it all in cash money. No checks."

Mac threw his head back and laughed. "Me too. I thought he was going to fall face-forward in his tuna salad sandwich."

"Good thing he had money in his safe."

"Truth be told, I would've taken less for the roots if he didn't have it. Better to get less than nothing at all."

The hike back to Wolf Valley was cold but went quickly, buoyed by their success selling the ginseng. "So," Blue asked as they neared Jewel Creek, "what do we do now?"

"You go home. I'll head to my parents' cabin. We can meet tomorrow and talk about how to divide the money."

"I don't want any of it."

Mac cocked his head and blinked. "What do you mean? You picked half. You get half."

"No. I want my share to go to the omegas too. They need it. It'll buy them blankets, get them extra rations of food and wood. They can buy medicine in town. Whatever they need. And the rest can go to setting up the ginseng farm. Just make sure the alphas don't find out about it."

"Damn it, Blue. Just when I think I can say you go your way and I'll go mine, you get all heroic on me."

Blue snorted. "Is that a compliment? Because I'm not sure."

"How's this?" Mac pulled him in and smashed their mouths together in a deep kiss. When he finally broke it, he leaned his forehead against Blue's. "Is that a better explanation?"

"Oh, yeah. That makes it all crystal clear." Blue chuckled, but his body was hardening, awakened by Mac's hungry kiss. "Don't go to your parents' cabin tonight. Come to my place. It'll be dark by the time we get back. Nobody will know."

"I don't know, Blue…"

"Please? Come on, Mac. I need you." He pressed against Mac, rubbing his cock against Mac's thigh. Its burgeoning thickness left no doubt how much he wanted Mac. "Fuck, don't make me beg."

Mac groaned but finally nodded. "Okay, you win. But don't say I didn't warn you."

CHAPTER 8

T he fire crackled in the fireplace and cast dancing light across the room. Blue's sparse cabin was toasty warm and seemed positively lavish after the weeks they'd spent roughing it in the forest. Near the fire was a large tub, filled now with steaming water. Mac sat in it, luxuriating in the heated water, letting it soak the cold from his bones.

Blue knelt by the tub, a bar of sweet-smelling hand-milled soap in his hand. He dunked it in the water, then rubbed it against a soft washcloth before he began to bathe Mac. Blue slid the soapy rag over Mac's shoulders and across Mac's back and chest. "Tell me this isn't preferable to the icy water in the creek."

"I never said I didn't like hot baths. I said they were impossible to get when you're camping out in the woods." He let his head hang forward so Blue could scrub the back of his neck. "It would take forever to heat enough water over a campfire to fill a tub like this."

"That's true. We could barely boil enough water for coffee in the morning!" Blue chuckled and rubbed more soap on the washcloth. The scent of honey and summer flowers tickled Mac's nose.

"Where'd you get that soap?"

"It was part of our rations."

"Huh. Omegas only get lye soap." He regretted saying it the moment the words left his mouth when the smile slid from Blue's face. "I'm sorry I keep bringing it up, Blue. I know you understand now, and I know it's not your doing."

"But I did nothing to stop it either, not even when I began to question the way things were."

"That doesn't mean it's your fault. Besides, we're going to change things now, right?"

Blue's lips tilted in a smile again. "Yes. With the money we got from selling the ginseng, the omegas will be able to buy whatever they need from the city. Fuck the rations. This winter, no omega freezes to death or starves."

"Right!" Mac slipped his hand behind Blue's neck and drew him in for a long, deep kiss. Then, without warning, he pulled Blue into the tub with him. Water sloshed over the sides onto the floor as the two of them filled the tub to over-flowing.

Laughing like children, they pulled themselves from the tub and dried each other off with the cabin's single towel. Still damp, they slipped beneath the blankets on the bed and cuddled for warmth. By the time they stopped shivering, they'd both fallen asleep.

* * *

LUC GROWLED and slapped the omega across the face, rocking the man's head back on his neck. "I'm only gonna ask you one more time. Where did you get that fucking money?"

"From Mac and Blue! I swear it, Luc!"

"Well, where did *they* get it from? And why would Blue give it to a fucking omega?"

The man shook in obvious fear. "I don't know! They gave some to a lot of people. Said we should buy blankets and extra food with it."

Luc pushed the man away from him, an expression of utter disgust twisting his face. He turned to JJ and Will. "Find Mac and Blue. I want to see them right now. And get this piece of shit out of my sight!"

A gust of icy air blew in when Will opened the door. The sky outside was leaden with the promise of more snow. JJ grabbed the omega and hauled him out of Luc's cabin, followed by Will. The door slammed shut behind them, abruptly cutting off the wind.

Luc threw the cash he'd taken from the omega onto the table, where it joined a messy spray of hundreds, all confiscated from omegas that very morning. When the rumor reached Luc's ears that some omegas had money, he sent his men on a cabin-by-cabin search. The raid yielded several thousand dollars.

He confiscated the money, of course. He'd have to think of a suitable punishment for the omegas who dared try to rise above their station and get more than they deserved. Half rations for winter, maybe. That'd teach them.

Turning his mind back to the root of the problem, he wondered again what Blue and Mac thought they were doing. Where were they getting the money? Were they printing the fucking stuff?

Luc didn't think so. The money didn't look counterfeit, and he doubted either one of them was smart enough to make fake bills that looked so real they could probably fool a banker. He slammed his hand down on top of the money.

"They stole it, maybe. Sure, that's it!" He felt a little better, the anger draining off, thinking he'd solved the mystery. "They went down to the city and held up a bank or something. Got to be." He scooped the money into neater piles. "I'm more surprised they didn't get caught, stupid as they are."

Still, that didn't answer the question of why they were giving it away. Luc sure as shit wouldn't give a penny of it to anyone, especially not the omegas. He was going to lock it away in the heavy black iron safe he kept in his bedroom. Maybe he'd get one of them smart phones he'd seen on the television.

Not that he had anyone to call, but that wasn't the point. It was the *having* that counted. As leader, he was required to have the best, the most. People expected it of him. It was his due as an alpha, just as nature intended. That's what his pa always said.

He felt a momentary wistfulness, thinking about his pa. They'd had to fight—it was the way of the pack—but he supposed he didn't actually have to *kill* his pa. He'd only had to best the old leader in a fight, but bloodlust took over. Then, when it was done, he realized he had to get rid of the rest of the old guard or risk someone challenging *him* for leadership.

Not everyone appreciated the change in management or the manner in which it changed. He'd had to exert himself to make sure everyone understood their place. Now, most people cowered when they saw him, which was just the way he liked it.

He turned his attention back to what was most important —the money. He got the bills stacked, then counted them. There were sixty-one hundred-dollar bills—six thousand dollars in total. That was more cash than he saw in an entire year, even *with* the leader's cut from the Standish logging operation and the sale of extra rations and supplies from the store.

That Blue Standish, a substandard alpha by anyone's measure even if he did whelp out of an influential clan, and Mac, an omega not worthy to lick Luc's boots, had managed to lay their hands on that much money irked Luc to no end.

He had it now, of course, but it didn't matter. *They'd* had it first, and that pissed him off. He wanted to know how they'd done it. Did they use weapons to hold a bank up? Or had they faked it, fooling the humans? He snorted. They probably walked into a bank with their fingers shoved into the pockets of their coats, pretending to have guns, and the humans fell for it. God knew the only thing more stupid than an omega was a human.

The door opened and Mac was thrust inside. JJ and Will stood behind him. All three were dusted with new snow, but it didn't hide their scrapes and swelling eyes. Mac's face was bruised and bloodied, and his hands were tied behind his back, but he must've put up a good fight before he was bound. He stumbled and fell to the floor on his knees.

Which was exactly where he should be, in Luc's opinion —crawling on his belly like a worm. *It's his own fault. When the pack leader calls, you either come quickly and quietly or face the consequences.*

Luc looked at JJ and Will. "Where's Blue?"

"Don't know. Might be with his folks or up at the logging operation. We found this one walking out by the omega cabins, and brought him here directly." JJ blew on his hands to warm them. "Fuck its cold out!"

"Stop complaining. You sound like an old woman." Luc returned his attention to Mac. "Where did you get it?"

"Get what?"

"I know you're an omega, but even you can't be *that*

stupid." Luc picked up a stack and shook it at Blue. "This! Where did you get this money?"

"I think the question is where did *you* get it?"

Luc gestured toward Will, who kicked Mac in the ribs. Mac grunted and rolled to one side.

"Never mind. I already figured it out."

"You did? I'm impressed. I didn't think you were that smart."

Luc snarled at Mac. "Shut up before I kill you where you lie!"

"Where did he get it, boss?" JJ asked. He cast a covetous gaze toward at the money Luc held.

Luc clutched the money tighter in his fist. "He stole it. That's how. Robbed a bank."

Mac sputtered, and at first Luc thought it was in anger, but after a moment, he realized Mac was laughing.

At him.

"God, your melon head is thicker than goddamn molasses left out in a snowstorm. How do you even manage to dress yourself in the morning?"

Luc bellowed in rage. "You know, I'm more than done with you. You should've died when my pa banished you, but I'm going to make sure you don't cheat your fate again." He turned his back on Mac and directed his orders toward JJ and Will. "Chain him up outside. If he doesn't freeze to death first, I'll pass sentence on him at sunrise."

"On what charges?"

Ha! He's not laughing now, is he? Luc turned back and glared at him. "You stole this money from the humans. What if they followed you back here looking for their money? You put the entire pack in danger, and for that, you're going to pay. You should never have lived to come back and cause us problems anyway. You know what? I think there's a good lesson to be learned here. There'll be no more banishment in this pack at all. From now on, if you're guilty of a crime, you die. That'll make everything simple." He thrust his chin toward JJ and Will. "I want everyone here at sunup, every single alpha, delta, gamma, and omega. I want everyone in this pack to witness what happens to traitors."

"You're wrong, as usual, Luc. I didn't steal that money! *You* did though. I came by it legally, earned it. It was mine, and I gave it to the omegas so they could buy more wood and supplies for the winter, but you stole it from them!"

Luc roared. "I'm the alpha! I'm the leader! *I* decide who gets what in this pack and who doesn't get shit. Not you. The omegas get enough to survive, and that's all they deserve!"

"You're a fucking scumbag, Luc. You always have been."

"Shut your lying mouth!"

"I'm not the liar here. *You* are."

"Yeah? You said you got the money legally. How? Did the humans just up and give it to you? Welcome to the city, Mac. Here's six thousand dollars. Enjoy."

Mac smirked. His right eye was swollen shut, and he could probably taste the blood on his lips, but his insolence was still abundantly clear. It made Luc want to smash Mac's face in, or better yet, to shift and rip the arrogant bastard's throat out.

"Nope. I just did something you were too stupid to figure out for yourself."

There was a glint in Mac's eyes—the one still open and not completely swollen shut, anyway—that sparked Luc's curiosity. Mac was telling the truth—he knew something Luc did not. He glanced at JJ and Will, then nodded toward the door. "Get out."

JJ grabbed the back of Mac's collar as if to haul him outside, but Luc stopped him. "No, leave him here. You two get out."

"W-what? But you said we should take him and—" JJ blinked at him, and Will looked equally confused.

"Get the fuck out!"

They exchanged a baffled glance but obeyed Luc, reluctantly returning outside to the coming storm. They were too well-trained to question a direct order from the leader, especially one as ruthless as Luc.

They might be dull, but they weren't complete idiots. They knew it could be them on the floor of Luc's cabin next, with their hands tied behind their backs, their faces beaten bloody.

Luc perched with one butt cheek, resting on the edge of his desk, arms folded across his chest. "What am I supposed to do with you, huh? It would be easier all around if you just told me what you did, Mac. Confess, and I give you my word your death with be painless and quick."

"Gee, what an offer."

"I can get the information in other ways, but none of them will make you very happy."

"What? You gonna torture me? Is that what the leader does now?"

"If I have to. I don't want to do it, believe me—torture is messy, but I'm not going let you die without finding out the truth about how you got your paws on that money."

"Why can't you just figure it out for yourself, genius? I mean, if a lowly omega could work it out, surely it won't be a problem for an almighty alpha."

Luc snarled and kicked out with his foot, catching Mac on the side of the head. "Tell me, or I'll slit your belly open and strangle you with your own intestines."

Mac had the audacity to smile. There was blood on his teeth. "Well, you can try."

Another kick laid Mac out flat on the floor.

"Fine. You stole it, but you don't want to admit it. You're

trying to make me think you're smarter than me, but it's all a lie. I'm not going to waste another breath on you." He stalked to the door and threw it open, barely feeling the gust of icy air in his fury. He yelled to JJ and Will, who were out on the lawn, rubbing their hands together over a fire burning inside a metal garbage can. "Take him out and chain his sorry ass to a tree. If he survives the night, I'll deal with him in the morning."

CHAPTER 9

Blue heard the whispers, and they cut through his heart like a hot knife through soft cheese. Luc had taken Mac, they said. Had beaten him and chained him to a tree like a dog. Everyone needed to show up at Luc's cabin at dawn, but not just to hear about a pack policy change. They were to witness Mac's execution.

Execution!

Since when did this pack give out death sentences? Banishment was the worst punishment ever meted out by the leader. Fights to the death between leaders and challengers sometimes happened, but they were accepted as collateral damage and not punishment. Had Luc completely lost what few brains he had rattling around in that gourd he called a head?

Execution. The word chilled Blue to the bone. Luc was going to murder Mac in front of the entire pack and call it justice. And for what crime? Mac had done nothing wrong. For imagined slights, for being smarter than Luc believed an omega should be? Because of Luc's jealousy and insecurity, a good man, a good wolf, was going to die.

Well, not if Blue had anything to say about it. Surely the other alphas would see the colossal mistake they'd be making if they let Luc use his bruised ego as a reason to kill an innocent man! Once the precedent was set, it would be all but impossible to reverse. This wouldn't stop with Mac's death. Every time somebody did something Luc didn't like or refused to do as Luc ordered, they'd be killed.

He stalked across the camp to his parents' cabin, head ducked against the whistling wind, and let himself in without bothering to knock.

His pa, Argyle Standish, was seated at the table. Also present was Blue's elderly uncle, the other owner of the Standish logging operation, Enoch. Plates of fried chicken and vegetables sat in front of them. His mother, Irvina, was seated across the way, lifting a steaming mug of tea to her lips when Blue burst inside.

"Blue! Where have you been, son? We've been worried." She smiled and gestured toward an empty chair. "Sit down, and I'll have Jane fetch you a plate." She snapped her fingers at the gamma servant girl who hovered in the background.

"I don't want to eat. I want to talk to you and Pa. You, too, Uncle Enoch. Please, sit down, Ma." Blue took the seat he'd been offered. "This is important."

Argyle put his fork down and watched Blue from under thick graying eyebrows. He looked more curious than concerned. "What's this about, son? Your brothers say you haven't been at the logging camp for a month. You know you're honor bound to put in your time overseeing the operation. What have you been up to?"

"Oh, your boy's just been tomcatting around, I reckon." Enoch laughed, a scratchy yet deep sound that reverberated in the cabin. "Don't you remember being his age and running after every piece of ass that wiggled in your direction?"

"Enoch! I'll have you know my son ain't no tomcat. He's a

good man. Responsible. Ain't that right, Blue?" Irvina huffed at her brother-in-law, obviously insulted anyone would think her boy was less than a chaste, upstanding member of the community.

"I know I haven't been up there, but I have a good reason, and I owe you an explanation, but it's a long story, and I don't have time to get into it right now. We have bigger problems to worry about. Have you heard what Luc has planned?"

Argyle held his hand up and looked toward Jane, who had her gaze cast down but was watching them from under her lashes. "Jane, you're dismissed. Go on, girl, get on home."

Jane nodded and silently removed her white apron, then hung it neatly on a peg near the stove. She took her worn and patched shawl from another peg and wrapped it around her thin shoulders. Opening the front door only wide enough for her to squeak through, she hurried out as if to minimize the cold she let into the warm cabin.

"Best if we talk without outside ears listening in. God knows those gammas like to gossip." Argyle picked up a chicken leg, and bit into it. Juice dripped over his chin, and he swiped at it with his sleeve. "Now, what's all this about Luc?"

"He's decided banishment is no longer a suitable punishment for serious infractions by omegas. He's going to start killing them outright."

Argyle's hand froze with the chicken leg an inch from his lips. "What?" He lowered the leg to his plate again, shaking his head. "Oh, you must be mistaken, Blue. No leader would kill a pack member outright except rarely in a leadership challenge or to protect another pack member. Not even an omega!"

Enoch speared a green bean on his fork and waved it Argyle. "Oh, I don't know, Argyle. Sometimes, situations take drastic measures to fix. Maybe Luc has the right idea. Most of the young 'uns have gone soft. Takes a hard man to be a good leader."

"Enoch, you know better than that. Killing is *always* a last resort."

Blue caught his father's gaze and held it, unflinching. "Luc and his men killed five alphas after he took over leadership of the pack. And then they killed the alphas' pups. What challenge did a child pose to Luc?"

His pa looked away. "That was different. It was a leadership change."

"Bullshit. No other leader felt it necessary to kill off an entire bloodline to secure his position. The pack has always taken care of its young. Orphans are never left to starve. Not even Gray Alden did that. Luc murdered his father and anyone who might've challenged Luc for leadership. Then he killed their children, and we did nothing but stand by and watch him do it."

Irvina gasped, her eyes wide. "Blue! Don't talk to your father that way!"

"I'm sorry, Ma, but it's the truth, and it's about time somebody said it out loud. We're wolves, and ruthlessness has its place, but we're people too. We're supposed to have compassion. Pa, haven't you always told me our function as alphas was to protect? How is letting Luc kill whoever he wants protecting anyone?"

When Argyle looked back again, his eyes looked haunted. Blue knew in that moment Mac had been right about everything. The alphas had forgotten their primary function in the pack, distracted from their purpose by greed and power. What's more, his pa knew it too.

"No other pack treats their own members this way. In the old country, the omegas were as valued as the alphas. The only difference was in the line of work each did. We had honor then. Something changed when our pack settled here, and it's been getting worse with every generation."

Irvina looked uncomfortable, her gaze flicking from Argyle to Enoch and back to her son. "Now, Blue, I think—"

Argyle looked thoughtful. "He's got some of it right, Enoch. The other packs I've been in contact with over the years aren't structured like ours. And our elders always told stories of a different way of life in the old country. Maybe he has a point."

Enoch growled. "He's still a pup, doesn't know his tail from his elbow."

Blue had enough of their discussion. They weren't getting the point. "Will you listen to me? Luc is going to kill Mac at sun up, Pa."

"Are you talking about McKenna Fuller? The omega? The one Gray Alden banished fifteen or so years ago? I heard he come back. Heard he got into trouble again too. Typical of an omega, huh?" Enoch snorted and bit off a piece of chicken leg.

Blue shook his head at his uncle's unrepentant prejudice and talked directly to his father instead. "Back then, Luc *lied* when he said Mac attacked him for no reason, Pa. Do you want to know what really happened that day? I was there, Pa. I saw it all. Luc got all over Mac's case, insulting him and his family until Mac snapped and challenged Luc to a fight. And Mac won, Pa. He won fair and square, had Luc down on the ground, belly up. Luc yielded, but when Mac let him go, all of Luc's friends attacked Mac. He couldn't fight them all off alone.

"When Mac came back to the settlement, Luc lied about the fight, and because Luc was an alpha, everyone believed him." Blue sighed and hung his head. "I feel guilty to this day that I didn't speak up back then. What happened to Mac was partially my fault too. I didn't attack Mac, but I didn't try to stop it either." He looked at Argyle. "I'm not going to let history repeat itself. This time, I'm not keeping my mouth shut. I'm not going stand by and let Luc ruin more lives."

Enoch poked a finger at him. "Blue, you listen to me, boy. Don't get involved. Speaking up against the leader of the pack is a good way to get yourself banished or worse. Ain't that right, Argyle?"

Blue ignored Enoch. "Pa, didn't you hear me? Luc isn't content with banishment anymore. He's going to kill Mac in cold blood come sun up. What makes you think he'll stop at killing omegas? If we let him do this, he'll start killing anyone who disagrees with him or even thinks about challenging him."

Enoch waved a hand at him. "Aw, that's horseshit!"

Blue slammed his fist down on the table, rattling the plates and drawing a squeal from his mother. "Damn it to hell, Uncle Enoch! I'm talking to my pa, not you. Why are you people so blind to the truth? How can you keep denying what's going on in this pack? It's been getting worse with each new generation of leaders. Maybe it's the mountain. Maybe there's something here that makes us lose our senses. I don't know. All I know is that you told me yourself that alphas are sworn to *protect* the weaker members, to *shelter* the pack. It's our function. The reason for our existence. How is letting a leader kill an omega for no good reason protecting anyone?"

He stood up and tried to draw in a calming breath but failed. Fury coiled in his belly like a snake tensed to strike. His fists clenched, and his jaw tightened. He couldn't ever remember feeling so angry as he looked back and forth between Argyle and Enoch. He had to fight the urge to shift as his wolf snarled just under his skin. "Pa, you're the head of the Standish clan, and Uncle Enoch, like it or not, you're his second. If you do nothing about this, if you refuse to take a stand against Luc, I'm done with you, done with this family. Done with this pack. I'll leave the mountain, if Luc doesn't kill me, too, that is."

Ignoring the halfhearted attempts by his mother for him to calm down and let cooler heads prevail, Blue turned on his heel and stalked out of the cabin. He glanced in the direction of the Alden place, knowing Mac was there somewhere, bleeding and bruised and chained in the snow like an animal, but there was nothing he could do for Mac at the moment. Not alone. Blue knew Luc would have his men watching Mac, and that they'd be armed.

Instead, Blue turned away and headed toward the omega cabins, his heart aching for the man he'd come to see as a person, rather than just an omega. The man who'd captured Blue's imagination and, ultimately, his heart.

"Don't worry, Mac. Hang in there, love. I'm going to fix this."

* * *

BLUE KNEW people were staring at him as he strode past the row of omega cabins, although they tried to be subtle about their interest. No one tried to stop him or even verbally acknowledged his presence. No one said hello or wished him a good day. Everyone knew who he was, but as an alpha, he was free to go where he pleased without question, and it wasn't their place to speak to him without being spoken to first.

He could feel their gazes burning at his back, though, and every so often, he picked up whispery snatches of conversation floating on the cold wind.

Alpha.

What's he doing down here?

Heard he tended Mac when he got beaten that time.

What's he want with us?

He ignored it all and pushed against the wind until he reached the last cabin on the row. It was shabbier than he remembered, and he felt another pang of guilt that Mac's family lived in such squalor while his own family lived in comparable luxury. He knocked on the door.

A small, pale face appeared in the crack when the door opened. Huge dark eyes looked up at him. He swallowed his anger and summoned a shaky smile for the child. "Hello. Are you Mac's sister?"

"Cousin." She had a slight lisp from a missing front tooth.

"My name is Blue. What's yours?"

"Amelia."

"It's nice to meet you, Amelia. Is your daddy home?"

She shook her head slightly. "Pa got kilt last year when a tree fell on him."

Blue felt his stomach lurch. "Oh. I'm so sorry. I—"

"Who's there, Amie? You're letting the cold in, child." A woman appeared behind Amelia and pulled the door open wider. She was an older woman, but the similarity between her face and Mac's was undeniable. He was the spitting image of his mother. "Oh, please forgive her, alpha. She don't mean to be rude. She's just a young 'un and don't know no better yet." She turned to Amelia. "When an alpha comes to the door, you let him inside, Amie. Right away, hear? You don't dawdle."

She opened the door and stepped aside. "Please come in. I'm Sylva Fuller. We ain't got much, but you're welcome to what we have."

"I'm not angry at her, Miz Fuller." Blue slipped inside and shrugged out of his coat. Amelia took it and hung it up on a peg behind the door. Half a dozen children looked up at him from where they sat on the floor draped with faded quilts and threadbare blankets. A few older teenagers and a pair of adults were gathered at a table placed near a potbellied woodstove.

The Fuller cabin was in bad shape. A pot sat on the floor in one corner, catching water made by melting snow dripping steadily from a hole in the roof. There was only one actual bed. It was placed against a wall. The mattress didn't quite fit right, showing springs on either side. It sagged in the middle, and it wasn't nearly wide enough to support more than one body. A couple of the windows were missing glass panes, and someone had taped plastic bags over them to try to keep out the worst of the cold.

Sylva began to give her brood orders. "Rudy? Make room next to the stove for the alpha. Clare? Put the pot on for tea."

A teenager with bright red hair jumped up from his seat, while a girl, nearly a woman, scurried to get the tea kettle from one of the burners on the stove.

"Please, Miz Fuller, I'm fine. I don't need anything."

"Come warm your bones, alpha." A gray-haired man gestured toward the chair recently vacated by Rudy. "I'm Angus Fuller, Mac's pa."

Blue nodded and seated himself on the surprisingly sturdy chair. The fire in the woodstove was small, but the heat felt wonderful. "Mac is in trouble, Mr. Fuller. Bad trouble." He glanced at the children, unwilling to say too much in their presence.

"Ain't nothing we keep from the pups, alpha. They need to learn the ways of the pack young if they want to survive."

"My name is Blue Standish, Mr. Fuller. Not alpha. Please, just call me Blue." He smiled his thanks as Clare handed him a thick, clay cup filled with an aromatic, steaming hot tea. It smelled good—peppermint, if he wasn't mistaken, with a little wild honey. He took a sip and proved himself right. "Luc Alden has taken Mac and plans to… Well, he plans to kill Mac when the sun comes up. JJ and Will are supposed to be spreading the word that Luc wants the entire pack there as witnesses."

A startled gasp drew his attention, and he look at Sylva. Her hand was pressed to her chest, and she'd gone as pale as little Amelia. "Kill Mac? Why? What did he do?" Her eyes, the exact color as Mac's, were wet with tears. "It's about the money, ain't it? I told Mac that money wouldn't do nobody no good. No alpha would let an omega get more than their due share of things. I told him—"

Angus interrupted her, his voice terse. "Sylva! Hush now." He nodded toward Blue. "Excuse her, alpha. She loves the boy, you understand. He was our firstborn."

"She's right." Blue saw astonishment brighten Angus's eyes. "About the alphas, I mean. And about the money. We should've known Luc would never allow it. Mac was just so set on it, I couldn't talk him out of it."

"You know what Mac did to get the money?" Angus's eyes widened.

"I helped him, Mr. Fuller. We hunted and dug the ginseng together, then took it down to the city to sell."

"I… I don't understand." Sylva sank onto a small three-legged stool Rudy carried over for her. "You knew? You helped? Then why is he in trouble? He was doing what an alpha ordered him to do."

Blue sighed. "It wasn't quite like that, Miz Fuller. It was Mac's idea. I was following his lead, not the other way around."

"But omegas don't lead!" Angus shook his head, obviously confused.

"Your son does, and he does a great job of it. Listen, the years he spent away from here changed Mac. He learned more, did more, saw more than any alpha of this pack could dream of, and one of the things he told me was that out there, in the human world, no one is better than anyone else.

Roles aren't carved in stone. Men born low can better themselves, and highborn men can fall. Women too. He said women are business owners, doctors, lawyers, all manner of things."

"And now he's going to die for it!" Tears slipped over Angus's craggy cheeks. "My boy is going to die for those high falutin' human ideas! The human world ain't the pack. He should've never come back here."

"Don't say that, Angus!" Sylva buried her face in her hands, her shoulders shaking as she sobbed. "I can't bear it!"

"That's just it, Mr. Fuller! I don't want Mac to die either."

"But we can't stop Luc. He's the leader!"

"Not for long. I have an idea, but I need your help. That's why I came here. Will you help me? Will you stand with me against Luc Alden? It may be the only way to keep Mac alive."

CHAPTER 10

Snow was falling as the pack began to assemble outside Luc's cabin. Voices were kept low, but they murmured about what was to happen and why they'd been summoned there in the cold and snow at the crack of dawn.

Blue had braved Luc's guards and given Mac a few blankets, for which Mac would be eternally grateful. They probably saved him from frostbite or worse. Only Blue's family's rank in the pack—second only to the Alden's—kept the guards from tearing the blankets away from Mac. Still, his hands and feet, bound with rope, were numb, and he couldn't stop shaking. His skin burned with the cold even as he tried to burrow deeper into the blankets.

He and Blue had been able to exchange a few whispered words when Blue gave him the blankets. Blue had a plan to gain him his freedom, although Mac highly doubted it would succeed. Still, it was better than nothing, he supposed. At least he wouldn't just stand there like a fear-frozen deer and let Luc kill him.

"Get him up!" JJ bellowed at the guards as he and Will stood sentry on either side of the door to the Alden cabin.

Rough hands pulled Mac to his feet and pushed him toward the porch. His bound ankles only allowed him to walk in awkward little hops, and he tripped and fell, but they yanked him upright again.

The door swung open and Luc stepped outside. He held a tall, wooden staff carved with wolf heads, the symbol of his rank as leader. He held it up, and silence fell over the pack. "You're all wondering why I've called you here this morning." He pointed the staff toward Mac. "This man, McKenna Fuller, is the reason. He's a traitor to us all!

"Fuller went down to the city and robbed a human bank. Then he came back here and tried to cast the blame for his crime on a few poor, ignorant omegas by giving them the money he'd stolen! What if humans had tracked him to Wolf Valley? They could've come up here and slaughtered us all, and why? Because McKenna Fuller is a greedy, no-account bastard. Because he learned to steal while he was living among the humans, and forgot what honor and loyalty mean. He forgot how to be a member of this pack, and he put all of our lives at risk!"

A low murmur rippled through the crowd as people began to comment on what they'd been told. A voice rang out above the buzz. "Where's the money now?"

Luc scowled, his gaze scanning the crowd. "Who said that?"

"Yeah, Luc… Where's the money?"

"The money. Who has the money now?"

"Shut up!" Luc's knuckles whitened around the staff, and he shook it in his mounting fury. This was not the reaction he'd anticipated. He'd thought the pack would be angry, but that it would be directed at Mac, not him. Yet here were people, alphas, no less, demanding to know what he'd done with the money. "The money isn't important. You're missing the goddamn point!"

An alpha named Peter Browne stepped forward. "I sure as hell think it is. What if the humans come looking for it? I've heard they're like a dog with a bone when it comes to their money. If he stole it from them, they're not just gonna up and forget about it."

"He didn't steal it!" Blue pushed through the crowd. Argyle Standish and Angus Fuller stood on either side of him. Both of the men held weapons—Angus held a pitchfork, and Argyle held an ax—and neither one looked happy. Their expressions were stony as they silently stared at Luc Alden.

"You shut up, Blue. Just because you're an alpha doesn't mean I can't punish you too." Luc bared his teeth at Blue.

"For what? Speaking the truth?" He turned toward the crowd. "We all know about the wild ginseng growing all over these mountains. It's illegal to harvest it on government land, but not on pack land. Well, Mac and I spent a few weeks harvesting it. Then we took it down to the city and sold it for top dollar. And why? Not for himself, not for me. We got it to give to pack members who need to buy extra food or blankets to survive the winter."

"Bullshit! Nobody believes that!" Luc laughed, but his voice died out as he realized nobody was laughing with him. "It's not true, I tell you! I'm an alpha. Mac is nothing but an omega! He's not smart enough to think of a plan like that!"

"Blue is an alpha, too, boss." JJ glanced at Luc.

"Blue is a piece of shit that sticks to the bottom of your boot!" Luc gestured wildly with the staff. "Now, you all listen to me. I'm the leader of this pack, and I say—"

"I'm glad you brought that up, Luc." Blue smiled. "Being leader of the pack, I mean. I think it's time we change that."

Luc's eyes flashed open wide, and his jaw hung open. "Are you seriously challenging me to a leadership fight, Standish? You? I'll have you on your back in thirty seconds flat!"

Blue grinned. "Well, you're right on one hand. This *is* a challenge for leadership. But I'm not the one issuing it."

Mac took a half step forward. "I am."

Blue nodded. "He beat you once before, Luc, and he'll do it again. Except this time, you're not pups anymore, and there'll be plenty of witnesses to see you go down."

The crowd muttered excitedly at the unexpected development, while Luc sputtered and cursed and worked himself up into a frenzy. He finally cracked the staff against a window, shattering the glass.

The sound of breaking glass seemed to stun the pack into silence. They stared at Luc, mouths open, waiting.

Luc held up the staff again. "This is ridiculous. He's an omega, for God's sake. I hereby pass judgment on McKenna Fuller and sentence him to death. JJ, get me an ax."

No one moved.

"JJ? Didn't you hear me? I said, get me an ax!"

JJ moved to one side. "Sorry, boss. A challenge has been put out. It's like, all official and stuff."

"He's an omega!"

"So?" Will moved over to stand by JJ. "Don't matter. Anybody can challenge for leadership. It's pack law."

"Well, I'm changing that pack law right now." Luc jabbed the staff toward Will and JJ, then turned and gestured toward the crowd. "Do you hear me? From now on, nobody but an alpha can challenge for leadership. How do you like that, McKenna? Huh?"

"You can't do that, boss." Will shook his head. "That law is the oldest one we got."

"Yeah, well, I'm leader and what I say goes." Luc was wild-eyed, his entire body visibly tensed.

JJ sighed and stepped off the porch. He pulled a knife out of his pocket and approached Mac.

"Wait!" Luc cried. "I get to kill him, not you! Step away, JJ." He took a step down off the porch.

JJ ignored Luc and bent and sliced through the rope binding Mac's feet. Then he went to work on the rope tied around Mac's wrists as well, freeing them. "It's on you, now, Mac. Best make good on your challenge."

Mac rubbed his hands, trying to get the blood flowing back in them. "Thanks, JJ."

Luc seemed beside himself, working up to a full-blown rage. "What are you doing? Are you crazy? Who told you to let him go?"

JJ threw Luc a sour look and turned his back.

Mac straightened his spine and lifted his chin. "Luc Alden, I formally challenge you for leadership of this pack. How do you answer?"

"I'm not lowering myself to fight a fucking omega!"

Blue took a step forward. "You either fight him, or you relinquish the leadership by default."

Luc's gaze skittered over the crowd as if desperately searching for someone, anyone to support him. None came to his aid. Instead, the omegas pushed forward through the crowd to stand with Mac. His family, Angus and Sylva among them, were first to move to his side.

"What's wrong, Luc? Nobody willing to stand with you against the pack now that there are witnesses here?" Blue gestured toward the crowd. "Where are the Alpha Ones now? JJ? Will? Anyone want to protest?" He pointed a finger toward Luc. "Mac beat you when we were pups, but your friends let you bully them into helping you because they were young and foolish, me included. After you ganged up on him, you brought him to your father. It was your word against his, and he paid the price for your lies. If he beats you today, there'll be no way to lie your way out of it. No one will risk their reputation or status by going against pack law. You will lose the leadership, and if you survive, you will no longer be an alpha."

"A-and if I win?" Luc seemed to calm himself and took a few steps toward Blue. The crowd parted around them, giving them space.

"Should you win, you remain leader."

"That's not good enough. If I win, he dies!" Luc turned and snarled at Mac, his hatred so blatant it practically crackled in the air.

Mac forced himself to remain expressionless, refusing to let Luc get under his skin. He stared stoically back at Luc, as unmoved as stone. "I agree."

Blue gasped. "Mac, what are you saying? That's not acceptable!"

"Sure it is. I'm already an omega. He can't demote me any lower than that, and we've already seen banishing me doesn't work. Don't worry, though—I don't plan on losing."

"No one ever does, Mac." Blue moved closer, although his gaze remained on Luc. "Don't agree to this. It's madness."

"Do you think I'll lose?"

Blue seemed to take a minute, and then his chin lifted, and he returned Mac's look with a confident one of his own. "No."

"Good. Then it's settled." He addressed Luc again. "You win, I die. I win, and you lose the leadership and will be demoted to omega."

"Sure, sure," Luc said. "I agree." Then, without warning, Luc swung the staff toward Mac's head.

Mac threw his arm up and blocked the blow. In the same motion, he wrapped his hand around the staff and yanked it out of Luc's grip, tossing it to the side.

Luc threw his head back, howling, and shifted, his clothing shredding around him. He snarled and snapped at Mac, but then turned and dashed through the crowd toward

Jewel Creek, his ears back and tail tucked between his legs. In a few minutes, he'd run to the tree line and disappeared into the forest.

Blue sidled up to Mac, grinning. "Well, we can't say we didn't see that coming."

"Nope. When you're right, you're right. I owe you a beer."

"I knew that little weasel didn't have the balls to stand against you in a fair fight." Blue bent down and picked up the staff. He offered it to Mac. "Well, here you go."

Mac blinked him and stared at the staff as if he'd never seen it before. "Huh?"

Blue pushed the staff against Mac's chest. "You're the new pack leader, Mac. You challenged Luc, and he conceded. Or rather, he ran off like the coward he is and lost by default."

No, no, no! He somehow hadn't quite thought about what the ramifications of him winning a fight with Luc would be. He'd just wanted to get out of the jam he was in. He had a life, plans, and they didn't include a pack of werewolves in the Appalachian Mountains. "Blue, I'm no leader. You take it. You're more equipped than I am to handle it. I've been gone too long."

The crowd around them was beginning to grumble, probably wanting to know why the new leader wasn't taking the staff of power, or whatever the fuck they called it, and tell them what to do next.

Blue lowered his voice and ducked his head. "That's not how this works, and you know it, Mac. Take the staff before we have a riot on our hands." He shoved the staff toward Mac.

Mac took it, albeit it reluctantly, and held it up over his head. The crowd yelled, and he realized the loudest cheers were coming from the omegas standing at the rear of the assemblage. *Oh, God, what have I gotten myself into?*

CHAPTER 11

Enoch Standish stood to the side of the crowd as McKenna Fuller, an omega, for God's sake, wrested the leadership of the pack from Luc Alden. Or rather, as Luc Alden handed it over to Fuller on a silver platter.

Fucking sniveling little coward, running off with his tail tucked between his legs like a goddamn pup. Enoch never liked Luc. He wasn't anything like his old man had been. Gray Alden had been a real leader, an alpha in the truest sense of the word. In fact, the only blind spot Gray ever had was Luc. In the end, it'd cost Gray his life.

Gray should've drowned that runt at birth.

Now look what'd happened. They had an omega as a leader! Luc might as well have cut all their throats while they slept.

Well, it wasn't going to stand, not while Enoch still drew breath. Shockingly, no one seemed inclined to challenge Fuller for the leadership. None of the younger alphas stepped up, not JJ, not Will—none of the Alpha Ones. He couldn't understand it. Didn't being alphas mean anything anymore?

How could they stand by and let an omega take the leadership staff?

Enoch couldn't issue a challenge for leadership himself, of course—he wasn't stupid. Fuller was much younger and far more muscular, and Enoch hadn't exactly been taking care of himself these last few years. He had a belly and got short of breath when he overexerted himself. He'd never be able to take Fuller hand-to-hand.

Blue sure as shit floats won't do it. He eyed his nephew with contempt. *I always knew there was something wrong with that boy. Look at him! Cozying up to an omega. It ain't right. It's almost like he—*

Enoch froze, his gaze flicking back and forth between Fuller and Blue. *Is it possible?* Revulsion rippled through him as his suspicion grew. *Shitfire! Why didn't I see it before? They're queer for each other!*

So that's what Blue was doing instead of working up at the logging camp. He was off sucking dick with McKenna Fuller. A small wicked smile curled Enoch's lips. *Well, the pack might be willing to have an omega as a leader, but how are they going to feel about having a faggot running things?*

People weren't likely to take Enoch's word on it, though. He'd need to get proof, but that shouldn't be too hard.

He was still smiling as he pushed through the crowd toward his brother's cabin.

* * *

THE CABIN UP at the logging camp looked pretty much exactly as it had when they'd last been there. It was cold inside; the stove hadn't been fired up in a while. Mac sat on the bed as Blue worked, loading kindling and tinder into the stove's belly and lighting it. Even so, he knew it would be a good, long while before the stove's heat would chase away some of the deep chill.

They'd come up to the cabin for one purpose only—to give themselves time to think and breathe. Ever since Mac accepted the leadership staff, he'd been inundated with requests, complaints, lectures, observations, and opinions from what seemed like every wolf in camp. Even the omegas were becoming more vocal, which he thought was a good thing, of course. But between their concerns about a more even distribution of rations and the demands of the gammas who didn't want to cook and serve food anymore and the deltas who didn't want to prepare the food and the alphas who didn't want to do much of anything and who thought the status quo should remain unchanged, he was losing his mind.

"Hey."

He looked up at the sound of Blue's voice. "Hey, yourself."

"You look like the weight of the world is on your shoulders."

Mac snorted. "It is. At least, the weight of this camp is. Everyone wants something, Blue. The alphas, the deltas, the gammas, the omegas... And nobody seems to want to pull their weight. Everyone seems to think I can just have someone else do their work."

"Nobody said it would be easy."

"I know. I'm not leadership material, that's all. I don't know what to tell everybody."

"We did this so the omegas would have a better life."

Mac shook his head. "No, you have it wrong. We picked and sold the ginseng so the omegas would have it easier. We challenged Luc because if we didn't, he was going to kill me."

"Ah, yes. Now I remember." A small smile played at Blue's lips.

Mac snorted and pulled Blue down onto the bed with

him. "You know, I don't know if I like this sassy new you. All puffed up because you had an idea that worked. You'd think you were an alpha or something."

Blue laughed and stole a kiss. "I am an alpha, and as such, I order you to strip off. You have way too many clothes on."

"Hey, you can't give me commands anymore. I get to give the orders. I'm leader."

"Only out there." He pointed toward the cabin window. "In here, we're equals."

"I have news for you. We're equals out there, too, now. If I do anything while I'm leader, it'll be to make sure of it. Now, as leader, I order you to get naked."

Blue threw his head back and laughed, then rolled off the bed and stood up.

"Hey, where do you think you're going?"

"You told me to get naked. The only way I know how to do that is to take my clothes off." He grinned at Mac as he began to strip. His shoes, socks, underwear, pants, and shirt flew in different directions. By the time he was done, Mac had shimmied out of his clothing as well.

Their bodies realized they were naked before their minds latched on to the fact, cocks hardening, balls swelling. Blue hopped on the bed again, and Mac threw his leg over Blue's, trapping him, slowly humping his hip. "Fuck you feel good. You smell good." He licked a wet path over Blue's shoulder. "You taste good."

Blue moaned and wrapped his hand around Mac's cock. "You feel pretty good yourself."

Mac sucked in a breath between his teeth. "You know what I really want?"

"What?"

"I want to fuck you."

"You're an omega, and you want to fuck an alpha?" Blue snorted and nipped at Mac's ear. "Okay."

Mac blinked. "Okay?"

"That's what I said, isn't it?" He kissed Mac, sucking on Mac's lower lip for a moment. "It's what I want too." He stroked Mac's length for another moment. "God, that's all I've wanted for a while now. This, in me, filling me up."

"Fuck, Blue."

"There's some lard in a can on the shelf by the stove. You better get it. We're going to need it."

Mac realized he was going to have to get up out of the warm bed to fetch the lubricant. It's a small price to pay, he decided as he scurried naked through the chilly cabin. Gooseflesh rose on his skin as he reached for the can on the shelf, then hurried back to bed. Diving under the covers, he held up the can like a fisherman holds a prize fish. "Got it!"

"I can see that. Now, put it down. You've got some work to do first."

"Yes, sir!" Mac happily obliged, ducking under the covers. He found Blue's dick with his mouth, already hard and wet with precome, and sucked it in. Tonguing the fat, round head, he teased even more wetness from it, sucking hard until Blue moaned and tried to pull away.

Mac was having none of it. He continued to suck until Blue's body arched and hot come spurted into his mouth. Only after he'd licked Blue clean did poke his head out from under the blanket. He reached for a kiss, letting Blue taste the come on his tongue, then grabbed for the can of lard.

Blue moaned again and then rolled to his stomach. He twisted his head, watching Mac from over his shoulder.

"Gonna fuck this beautiful ass." Mac gave Blue's bottom a light slap, then kneaded the firm flesh. "Gonna fuck you right into the mattress."

Blue didn't answer, but his butt rose up a bit and his breathing grew a little harsher. A low sound that might've been a growl rumbled low in his chest. It was sexy as fuck.

Mac opened the can and scooped out a healthy dollop of white lard. He tossed the can to the side, and then slid his slick fingers between Blue's ass cheeks. When he had the crack well-coated, he felt for Blue's hole.

Blue's body was tight, clenching around his finger as he tried to work the lard in. Hot and silky, Blue's channel molded around his finger, squeezing it, melting the grease into a slick, slippery mess. His finger made wet sounds as he fucked Blue with it, sliding it in and out of Blue's ass.

A second finger slipped in beside the first, stretching Blue, readying him for what was to come. Mac's cock, hard and aching, beaded with precome as he absently rubbed it against Blue's thigh.

His body burned with need as he withdrew his finger and positioned himself above and behind Blue. Pressing the head of his cock against Blue's hole, Mac pushed in. Slowly—God knew he wanted to slam himself home, fuck Blue hard and fast until they both lost consciousness, but he forced himself to take his time so he would cause Blue as little discomfort as possible. He inched his way inside, centimeter by torturous centimeter, pausing frequently to allow Blue's body to adjust to the intrusion.

It seemed like forever but was probably only a few long minutes before he was completely seated inside Blue's body. He rested, concentrating solely on feeling, on experiencing how it felt to have Blue wrapped around his cock. It was amazing, he decided, more so than he ever remembered it being with anyone else. Was it just because Blue was a wolf like him that made it feel so extraordinary? Made him feel as though their souls were connected as well as their bodies? Or was it because of something else, some deeper feeling he had for Blue?

Maybe it was both. *Yes, definitely both,* he decided. He held his breath and waited for Blue to relax. Then he moved, and the world shifted on its axis.

Anticipation swelled within him like steam in a boiler, pressure building, looking for an escape. His thrusts gained momentum, his hips rhythmically slapping against Blue's ass until the heat growing in his balls and belly finally reached critical mass. His climax hit him like an avalanche, an unstoppable force he couldn't hope to stand against.

Not that he wanted to even try.

Afterward, he slipped free from Blue's body and got up to fetch a cloth. He wet it with water from a pot on the stove, now warm from the fire, and carried it back to Blue. Without saying a word, he gently cleaned Blue up, then wiped himself down.

"Hey." Blue's voice was soft and breathless. "How was it?"

Mac smiled and leaned in for a soft kiss. "Amazing. Did I hurt you?"

"Nah. Never did that before though. Not on the receiving end, I mean. I don't know if I would like it with anyone else. With you, though... It was amazing. I mean, it's hard to describe, but it filled this need I didn't even know I had."

"So, we're good?"

"Oh, honey, we're more than good. We're golden."

Mac lay down next to Blue and let the weariness of the day and the contentment of the past few minutes lull him. His eyes drifted closed, and when he fell asleep, it was with Blue nestled in his arms.

CHAPTER 12

Enoch had been tentatively casting out feelers for men who might be interested in working with him to challenge Fuller for leadership. He planted seeds for the rumor mill about Fuller being queer, although he kept Blue's name out of it. If people thought Blue was queer, then maybe others in the Standish clan were that way? Guilt by association was not something he was willing to risk.

So far, no one was willing to take an open stand against Fuller. There was too much support for Fuller, too many uppity omegas thinking they had the right to an opinion now, the right to dissent. There was no telling what they might do if someone challenged Fuller for leadership in the traditional sense—there might be an omega uprising, and then where would they be? Who would do all the manual labor? Everyone's lives would be disrupted.

He eventually realized he needed to change his plans. Enoch decided the easiest and safest thing to do was simply kill Fuller. Nobody could lead if they were dead, right? As soon as Fuller's death was revealed, someone would have to step in and take up the staff. This time, it wouldn't be a fucking omega either. It would be someone with experience, strength, and wisdom, someone who understood that the old ways were best for everyone involved.

Someone like himself, for example.

As soon as Fuller's body was discovered, Enoch would take up the staff and declare his intention to be leader. Any challengers would be swiftly dealt with, and not by hand-to-hand combat either. No, Enoch knew he couldn't win against an able-bodied younger man. He'd have his supporters simply shoot whoever disputed his claim.

And he had no shortage of followers now. In fact, he had more than he could possibly use. The fact that he offered good money brought men out of the woodwork, all pledging their undying loyalty to him. More than once he'd silently thanked Luc Alden for being such a greedy bastard. After all, it was Luc's money that was funding Enoch's plan.

After Fuller took up the leadership staff, Enoch had gone into Luc's cabin and found the safe. The combination hadn't been difficult to figure out—Luc was as dull as mud and his father hadn't been much brighter. The combo was Gray Alden's birthday—eleven, eighteen, nineteen, six, five. He'd popped the safe open in no time.

Inside were thick stacks of bills. It seemed it was the Aldens' habit to squirrel away cash money, to the tune of roughly twenty thousand dollars, an amount that surprised even Enoch, who was well aware of the Alden family's greed. More than enough to buy the loyalty of as many men as Enoch needed in order to see his plan succeed. He'd stuffed his pockets full, then left the cabin.

Now all he needed was to find some way to get Fuller alone and away from camp. He had to be killed somewhere up on the mountain and left for the hunters to find. Maybe make it look like an accident. Yeah, that would work. Fuller was banished when he was just a teenager, hardly more than a pup. He basically grew up with humans. He probably didn't know the first thing about surviving in the wilderness, and his wolf instincts were most likely so rusty from disuse they'd be worthless to him. It was totally believable that he could fall down a ravine and break his neck or get trampled by wild boar or mauled by a bear.

But how to get him up on the mountain alone?

The solution was almost ridiculously obvious.

Blue. Enoch would use Blue to lure Fuller up onto the mountain. They were queer for each other, right? He was booking on them having feelings for one another. He couldn't understand how two men would want to fuck each other, but he knew it happened, and they even got married in the human world. From the way he'd seen Blue and Fuller look at each other, Enoch understood he was on to something.

He'd kidnap Blue and leave a trail for Fuller to follow. Then, when Fuller came to rescue Blue, he'd kill them both.

He felt a little regret at having to kill his nephew, but they all had to make sacrifices, didn't they? Besides, with Blue gone, he no longer would have to worry about having a faggot in the family tarnishing the Standish name.

No one could ever find Blue's body, of course. Everyone would have to believe Blue left the camp, maybe even killed Fuller himself in a fit of jealousy or something.

Wait a minute! That's perfect! I can make it look like a murder-suicide. After it's done, I'll have my men spread word of a terrible fight Blue and Fuller had over leadership of the pack, and let everyone believe Blue killed Fuller and then himself. Enoch chuckled, pleased with himself and his idea. *And I don't have to trouble myself staging an accident or bear mauling—all it's going to cost me is the price of a couple of bullets. Easy peasy. I can even have the pleasure of shooting Fuller myself.*

Finding them wouldn't be a problem—he'd had them

followed by one of the more experienced trackers on his payroll. They were staying at the Standish cabin up by the logging camp. He wasn't surprised. It was a perfect place for an illicit tryst. Hardly anyone went up to the old cabin anymore, hadn't for years. He was shocked it was still standing.

Tomorrow, he decided. *Tomorrow Fuller dies, and I become leader of this pack.*

His decision made, he ordered his gamma servant girl to make him a sandwich. He ate quickly and then left his cabin, suddenly excited to set his plans in motion.

* * *

BLUE YAWNED AND STRETCHED, arching his back. He scratched his nuts, then followed his nose to the stove where a pot of coffee percolated. After pouring himself a cup, he glanced around the cabin.

Mac was gone already. He'd said he was going to the omega cabins to talk with his folks and a few others about a plan to redistribute the money from the ginseng sale to everyone. Which reminded Blue—he'd promised to go to Luc's cabin and fetch the money back. It was probably in the safe in the back of the cabin. God knew what the combination was—probably something as obvious as Luc's birthday, or his father's maybe. After all, it belonged to Gray Alden before Luc inherited it.

First things first—he needed to pee. Then more coffee, followed by a quick sponge bath in heated water. He smelled, and his hair needed washing. Then he'd get dressed and hike down to the settlement to Luc's cabin. Maybe stop and say hello to his folks. He hadn't seen them since his argument with them when Luc took Mac captive, and felt bad about the way he'd left things between them. Maybe it was time to mend fences, especially since his dad and uncle Enoch had stood by him when he faced Luc.

He downed his cup, then hurried outside to pee, returning as quickly as possible. It was bitterly cold, and he had nothing on but the skin he was born in. He went to the stove, shivering, and poured himself another cup of steaming hot coffee. He stirred a teaspoon of sugar into it, taking it black as usual. *Whew! Mac sure made it strong this morning.* He added more sugar to combat the bitterness and took another sip. *Better.* The double dose of caffeine zinged through his system, perking him up.

After he'd finished his second cup, he put a pot of water on the stove to warm and rooted around in the cupboard for something to eat. There was a can of tuna fish, a jar of put-up pickles, and an unidentifiable tin without a label. He settled for a few handfuls of dry cereal they'd brought up with them. *We really need to stock up if we're going to spend much time here. We can't survive on Cheerios, for God's sake.*

By the time he was done, the pot of water was steaming. He brought it to the table along with a washcloth and a bar of soap and set about making himself smell good again. Or at the very least, a little less rank. After washing his hair, he felt the chill in the cabin more acutely and got dressed.

Taking the pot, he opened the door to toss out the used water and was surprised to see his uncle, Enoch, walking up the path to the cabin. "Uncle Enoch? What are you doing up here?"

"Oh, hey, Blue. I didn't think anyone would be up here. I was thinking about your cabin and realized I hadn't been up here in a while. I came to see if any repairs needed to be made." Enoch followed Blue into the cabin. "What are you doing here?"

Blue hemmed and hawed, not quite knowing how to frame an answer. *Mac and I come up here to screw our brains out* didn't seem an appropriate response, even though it was true. "I like the solitude sometimes. And you know, I had that disagreement with my folks, so I didn't really want to stay home either."

"Ah, yes. About that. Funny you should mention it. I was just talking to your father yesterday, and he said he wished you would come home so he could speak to you about it. I got the feeling he wanted to apologize. You know, for not believing you about Luc."

Blue smiled. "That's real good to hear. I was actually going to go down there today."

"Excellent! I can see the cabin is in decent shape, so I'll walk down with you, all right?"

"Sure. I can use the company. Just let me put my boots on."

Enoch smiled at him and nodded. When Blue was ready to go, Enoch motioned gallantly toward the door. "Please, after you, Blue."

"Why, thanks, Uncle Enoch." Blue grinned and opened the door.

The last thing Blue expected was for someone to be on the other side, nor did he expect a rolled-up sock to be shoved in his mouth or a black hood to be pulled down over his head. It all happened so quickly, he didn't even have the presence of mind to fight or shift. By the time he did, his hands and feet were tied and he was on his back.

"Okay, boys. Grab his feet and hands and let's go. It's a hike up to the spot I've got in mind."

Uncle Enoch? What is this, some sort of sick joke? He struggled as he felt himself picked up by wrist and ankle, and semi-carried off the porch and across the yard. His back and butt scraped the ground, and he knew if they went any substantial distance, he probably wouldn't have much skin left on either.

He tried to yell, but they'd stuck the sock in his mouth so deeply he'd gagged on it.

What in the blue hell was Enoch thinking? Why was he doing this? Blue didn't have anything of value. The money from the ginseng was locked up in Luc's safe. He certainly didn't have any power. He wasn't pack leader—Mac was.

Mac.

Oh God.

It came to him like a lightning bolt in his brain. Enoch knew about him and Mac and what they'd been doing together up at the cabin. Somehow, Enoch had found out how they felt about one another.

Enoch wanted something from Mac and was going to use Blue to get it. But what?

Then he knew.

The only thing of value Mac had that could possibly interest Enoch was the leadership staff. Enoch wanted to be pack leader, and the only way he could get was to fight the current one. Except Enoch was going to cheat.

He was going to ambush Mac and kill him, and he was going to use Blue to lure Mac up onto the mountain.

Blue thrashed, arching and twisting his body like a madman, trying to shake his handlers loose. If he shifted now, he risked breaking a leg or worse, but he was just about ready to risk anything. Before he could, a hard blow to the head made his decision for him and the sweet oblivion of darkness fell on him.

CHAPTER 13

"Mac! Mac come quick!" Mac looked over at the sound of his name being called. He'd been visiting with his ma and pa and had taken his leave of them. He'd been walking between the rows of omega cabins, hoping to get back to Blue's cabin before noon when Thatcher, a delta, ran up the path toward him. "Whoa, what's wrong?"

"It's Blue. He's hurt. He's hurt real bad!"

Mac's stomach sank to his feet and he grew lightheaded. "What happened? Where is he?"

Thatcher tugged on Mac's arm, urging him to follow. "He's up on the mountain. Come on!" He set off at a trot, with Mac in hot pursuit.

"What's he doing up on the mountain?"

"I don't know. He said something about hunting. There's blood everywhere!" Thatcher put on a fresh burst of speed, forcing Mac to push to keep up.

Mac's heart was pounding with a combination of fear and exertion by the time they reached a point where Thatcher finally slowed down. He skidded to a stop and bent over at the waist, panting for breath.

Mac gasped for air as well and tried to massage a cramp out of his calf. "Where is he? I don't see him."

Thatcher pointed toward a ravine about forty feet away from where they stood. "There. That's where he is. He fell over the edge."

Mac hurried toward the gulch. He approached the edge, which looked crumbly and unstable, and forced himself to slow down. Inching his way forward, he peered over the rim of the steep drop. "Blue? Where are you? Blue, answer me!"

A sharp white-hot pain hit him in the back with the force of a hard-swung baseball bat, and stars danced across his vision. The pain exploded within him like fireworks, bright and hot, stealing the breath from his lungs and the vision from his eyes. His legs gave out and he toppled over the edge of the ravine, but darkness swallowed him before he hit the bottom.

* * *

BLUE HEARD the gunshot and cringed, but no pain followed the sound. Whatever was being fired upon, it wasn't him.

He almost wished it was. His back was rubbed raw, burning and throbbing like hellfire, and he was sure there was a trail of his skin leading from the cabin all the way up the mountain.

His energy was nearly sapped. He felt exhausted, pissed off, and scared shitless all at the same time. Not for himself— for Mac. Mac didn't deserve anything of this. It was all Blue's doing. He'd been the one to convince Mac to take the staff.

Whoever was carting him up the mountain finally dropped him. Pain from his raw back lanced through him, and he cried out against the gag. Fuckers! When he got out of this—and he was sure he would, somehow—he was going to skin them all and see how they liked it.

Then he heard Enoch's laughter, and something in it chilled Blue to the bone. He froze, listening hard for some clue, some indication who or what had been shot, and prayed harder than he ever had before that it hadn't been Mac.

"Well, well, little nephew. I'm sorry about all this, I am, but it couldn't be helped. Really, when you think about it, this is all your fault anyway. You had to go get all queer with Fuller. If you hadn't been so perverted, I wouldn't have needed to get rid of you, too, but I can't have people thinking their new pack leader has a fucking fairy in the family."

Blue bit down hard on the sock, screaming around it, trying to make himself understood. *You cocksucking bastard! What did you do to Mac? What did you do?*

"Oh, I suppose you're asking about your—what do they call them these days? Fuck buddy? He's dead. Shot him right in the back. Oh, you should've seen it! He was crying out your name, thinking you were dead at the bottom of the gully. Such a pathetic omega bastard."

Tears squeezed out the corners of Blue's eyes. If he thought he was in pain before, it was nothing compared to the overwhelming, heart-stopping agony that coursed through him after Enoch told him Mac was shot. *Not dead though. He's not dead. I refuse to believe he is.* He yelled against the gag again. *I'm going to kill you when I get free, Enoch. I'm going make it painful too. And slow.*

Enoch lifted his gun, a .22, and aimed it at Blue's head. "One quick shot and you'll be dead before you hear the bang."

Fury and fear were a potent combination, and Blue's self-control was lost to it. He shifted, whimpering when one of his rear legs twisted painfully against the ropes binding him.

"Aw, shit. Hold still, Blue." The gun in Enoch's hand shook a bit. "You keep moving and I'm likely to shoot you in the leg instead of the head. Then it'll be more suffering for you and more wasted bullets for me."

Blue snarled at him and tried to ignore the pain, continuing to work to free himself from the cords. He only succeeded in twisting them around his body.

A shot cracked, echoing around him, and a small clod of dirt next to his head erupted, coating his face with bits of earth. *Shit! That almost hit me!* Somehow, he hadn't quite believed Uncle Enoch would attempt to kill him. They were family, for God's sake! He howled and redoubled his efforts to free himself from the ropes.

"Oh, well, fuck. I don't have time for this nonsense." Enoch scowled at him, the hand holding the gun hanging loosely at his side. "I got to get back down to the settlement and claim leadership." He turned to one of the men standing nearby. "I suppose it ain't right for a man to shoot his own kin anyway. Griff? Here, you take my gun. Give me some time to get off the mountain and then put one in his head. Make it clean, hear?" He glanced down at Blue. "After he's dead and shifts back to his man-self, put the gun in his hand. Got to make it look like he killed Fuller and then himself. Come on down to the settlement when you're done."

Enoch walked off, followed by the rest of his men. Blue lay on the ground panting, exhausted by his efforts to free himself, his rear leg throbbing with pain. He shifted back into his man-self, the pain traveling with him from form to form. "You really gonna do his dirty work for him, Griff?"

Griff kept the gun trained on Blue. "Best if you don't talk. Only got to wait a few more minutes; then I'll put you out of your pain."

"Come on, Griff. We've known each other since we were pups. You were never a bad guy."

"Yeah? I'm a delta. I wasn't good enough to hang around

with the Alpha Ones, including you, Blue. Don't lie there acting like we was best friends."

"Maybe so, but I never tried to shoot you!"

"Just because you never had the chance before don't mean you'd never do it."

"That's ridiculous. Besides, we're not kids anymore. We're grown men. Why are you doing this? Why are you helping Enoch?"

Griff sniffed and shook his head. "Things aren't ever going to be the same with an omega as leader. It ain't right. It goes against the natural order." He smirked. "Besides, Enoch pays real good."

Blue felt desolation ripple through him in an icy wave, leaving him numb. "Enoch *paid* you? Where'd he get the money?" He closed his eyes and groaned as he answered his own question. "Of course. He found the ginseng money."

"The what money?"

Blue opened his eyes just in time to catch movement from over Griff's shoulder. He stuttered, trying to keep Griff's attention focused on him. "Um, ginseng. You know, the plant? It grows wild around here. Humans pay top dollar for it, if you can find it. We, me and Mac, found a bunch and sold it down in the city. We gave it to the omegas, but Luc took the money from them, and now I guess Enoch has it. Tell me, how much did he pay you?"

Griff puffed out his chest, looking smug. "A lot. A hundred dollars cash money."

Blue barked out a harsh laugh. "Is that all? Oh, man, Griff. Enoch just took you for a ride. Do you know how much he's sitting on right now? Thousands. *Thousands!* And he only paid you a miserable hundred to commit murder for him?"

He could see Griff's expression morph from superior to surprised. "You serious? You wouldn't be lying to me, would you? I mean, I still have to shoot you, Blue. I gave my word. You understand."

The shadowy movement behind Griff was closer now. "Oh, sure, sure. I completely understand. You have to worry about your honor and all. Don't want Enoch spreading it around the settlement that you welched on an agreement. But I'm not lying. It's all true. He has thousands of dollars from the ginseng sale. Plus, who knows how much money Luc and his father had put away. Enoch probably has that money too."

"And that stingy rat bastard only paid me a lousy hundred bucks!" Griff scowled. His face flushed, red creeping up his neck and across his cheeks. "Him and me, we're gonna have words when I get down off the mountain." He nodded at Blue. "I do appreciate your telling me, Blue. Now, close your eyes, and let's get this over with."

"Wait!" Blue scrambled, trying to find something else to say to keep Griff from pulling the trigger. "I, uh... I have some last words. I mean, that's proper, right? A condemned man gets to speak a few last words? Like my will and testament, you know."

Griff rubbed the side of his face with the barrel. "Well, I reckon. But make it quick, okay? I want to be off the mountain in time for supper."

"Sure, sure. Um, to my ma and pa, I leave the cabin up at the logging camp and everything in it—"

"Uh, don't that already belong to them? I thought your family owned that cabin."

"No, it's mine. I built it with my own two hands."

Griff nodded. "Oh, okay. Is that it?"

"No, no. I got my collection of squirrel tails I wanna leave to my baby sister, Renee. She always liked them fluffy tails. And there's my books. Let's give them to Uncle Floyd. He always did like to read. Now, you tell my folks there's a box of stuff under my bed at the cabin that they should just throw away. Don't look through it—it's private man-stuff. You know what I'm saying. Tell my pa not to let my ma see it."

Griff cackled. "You dog! You got dirty magazines up there?"

Blue thought about the few gay porn magazines he'd managed to get mailed to a post office box down in the city, and nodded. "Yeah, just that."

There was a dull thudding sound, and Griff's expression shifted into one of comical surprise. Then his eyes rolled up in his head and he slumped to the ground.

Mac stood behind him, a large rock in his hand.

"Jeez, what took you so long? You sure took your time getting over here." Blue wiggled against his ropes. "Get me out of here, will you?"

"Sorry. I had to find a big enough rock without him noticing me. Also, there's this little matter of me having been fucking *shot*." Mac bent over, quickly searching Griff's pants. He pulled out a small pocketknife and used it to make short work of Blue's bonds.

BLUE HAULED himself to his feet, immediately looking for Mac's injury. "Where did he shoot you?"

"In the back. Your uncle is a fucking coward, Blue. No offense."

"Oh, no offense taken. I agree with you. Let me see." He gently urged Mac to turn around. "Thank God it was only a .22. Looks like it went clean through." The entry was just behind Mac's shoulder blade, and the exit just under his collarbone.

"Yeah, I don't think it even nicked bone. Hurts like a bitch though. I've got to get down to my ma. She's helped heal more injuries than the delta doc in the settlement. She'll set me to right in no time."

Blue nodded, then glanced at the ground. Strips of his shirt and pants lay there, destroyed when he'd shifted back and forth from his wolf-self. He picked one up and used it to staunch the flow of blood from Mac's wound. Then he took the largest piece of fabric from his shirt he could find, and wrapped it around Mac's shoulder, passing it under Mac's arm and tying it in a knot on top. "There. It ain't much, but it's the best I can do for now. Let's go. I don't want to get caught working our way down in the dark."

"Hey."

"What?" He looked into Mac's blue eyes. They looked bright and a little teary.

"I'm really glad Griff didn't shoot you."

Blue's mouth tilted in a half smile. "Yeah, well, I'm glad Enoch's aim wasn't any better."

When Mac slipped his hand behind Blue's head and pulled him in for a kiss, Blue was more than willing to comply. Their kiss was soft but tinged with hunger and reflective of all the emotions warring inside Blue at the moment—anger at his uncle, apprehension of what was going to come next for them, fear that he'd nearly lost Mac, relief that he hadn't, and a fierce sort of joy that came from being kissed by the man he cared deeply about.

Unnoticed by them, a pair of yellow eyes watched from a screen of brush as they began the long trek down the mountainside. After a few minutes, Luc Alden followed behind them.

CHAPTER 14

"Oh my God, McKenna! What've you gone and done to yourself now?" Sylva cried out when she opened the door and saw her blood-soaked son standing on the cabin stoop. She hustled him inside, paying almost no mind to Blue aside for a short nod, even though all Blue wore was a cluster of leaves held in front of him for modesty. Everyone in camp was used to nudity—it was a byproduct of shifting.

Blue followed them inside and closed the door behind him.

"I got shot, Ma. Can you help?" Mac groaned as he sat down on the three-legged stool at the table. "I think it went straight through. Just need some patching, I think."

"You ain't been home but a couple of moons, and you've done got beat up, beat down, and shot." Sylva clucked her tongue at him as she examined his wound. "It don't look so bad. I don't think the bullet nicked anything important. A couple of stitches and you should be right as rain."

Blue limped over to a chair by the fire and smiled at Amie who sat on the floor playing with a rag doll.

"Blue's hurt too, Ma."

Blue waved off Mac's concern. "Aw, no, I'm fine. Just twisted my leg is all. Go on and take care of Mac. We got things to tend to as soon as he's ready."

"As you wish. You wrap yourself up in that quilt there before you catch your death, alpha."

"My name's Blue, and much obliged, Miz Fuller." Blue wrapped the worn, hand-stitched quilt around his shoulders, grateful for its warmth.

Sylva set about gathering her supplies—a small jar of clear liquid, a needle, thread, and a clean piece of fabric to use as a bandage. She opened the jar and dipped a corner of the fabric into it. "This is going to sting, son."

"Is that Pa's 'shine? Give it here, Ma." Mac held it under his nose and sniffed. "Damn! He still makes the most powerful 'shine in the mountains, doesn't he? I remember sneaking sips when I was a kid."

"Hmph. This jar ain't for drinking. I use it to clean the wounds of people who have the poor sense to get theirselves shot." She took it back and screwed the lid back on.

"Aw, Ma, I couldn't help it. Enoch Standish shot me in the back."

"What? That coward!" She bit her lip and flushed red, her gaze casting to where Blue sat, watching. "My apologies, alpha. I know Enoch's your kin, but it's true. Any man who shoots another in the back is plum yellow."

"No apology necessary. I'm the first to agree with you, and I swear I'm going to see my uncle pay for what he did to Mac. And please, just call me Blue."

She nodded. "I'd appreciate it if you'd see he don't get no more holes put in his hide."

Mac winced as Sylva stitched the wound on his back closed. "Where is Pa, anyway?"

"Down at the omega store. We needed our rations of flour and coffee."

"That's something we should talk about, Mac. We don't need four separate stores. Why can't the alphas, deltas, gammas, and omegas all get their rations from one place?" Blue rubbed his sore leg, trying to sooth the ache.

"Amie, get the alpha some of Pa's liniment for his leg. You put some of that on your leg, alpha, wherever it hurts. Rub it in good. It'll help."

"Thanks, Miz Fuller. I appreciate it." Blue didn't bother to ask Sylva to call him by his first name again. He'd done that several times already, and she refused. She just couldn't seem to overcome a lifetime of training.

After a few minutes, Sylva bit off the end of the thread with her teeth and sat back. "There. That's as good a job as I can manage."

"It's fine. Thanks, Ma." Mac leaned forward and kissed her cheek. "You're still my best girl."

Sylva blushed and waved him away. "Oh, go on with you, McKenna Fuller. You save that for some pretty young thing." She stood up and returned her needle and thread to a small box on the mantel. "You boys sit by the fire and relax. I'll get supper ready."

"We can't stay, Ma. We have to go find Enoch." Mac started to stand up, winced, then straightened all the way.

Blue had a corner of the quilt folded up to expose his leg, and was rubbing liniment into the muscle. It reeked to high heaven, but he could already feel soothing warmth penetrating deep. "Yes'm, that's right. Enoch nearly killed Mac. I can't let him hurt anyone else."

Sylva leveled a meaningful look at Blue. "Well, you look after my boy, alpha. He don't deserve to be hurt no more." He got the distinct impression she knew *he* was the *pretty young thing* she'd mentioned earlier, and getting shot wasn't the sort of hurt she meant.

He sat up straighter and tried to forget he was wearing nothing but a quilt. "Yes, ma'am. I will."

Sylva motioned to her niece. "Amie, go fetch a pair of trousers and a shirt from the trunk yonder." She looked back at Blue. "They ain't much, been handed down a time or two and mended lots, but they're clean and they'll do you until you get to your own clothes."

"Again, I'm much obliged, Miz Fuller."

He hurriedly dressed in the pants and shirt Amie gave him. Sylva was right—they were worn and practically more patches than original fabric, but they were dry, warm, and fit him well enough. He wondered if they'd belonged to Mac or one of his brothers. Probably all of them at one time or another, he realized.

"Mac, I want to stop up at my cabin before we go after Enoch." He gestured toward his clothing. "I got extra clothes up there."

Mac looked at him and snickered. "You do look a little like a pup dressing up in his pa's clothes. Okay. We should hurry though. I don't want Enoch to get too comfortable thinking he's going to be leader."

They bid goodbye to Mac's family, then hiked up to the logging operation and Blue's cabin. Blue hurriedly searched through a stack of clothing in the bedroom, letting his nose sort out the clean from the dirty. Finally, he chose a blue plaid shirt and a relatively clean pair of jeans.

"Ready?"

Blue held up a hand. "Wait a minute. Maybe we ought to arm ourselves, Mac. Last time we met up with Enoch you got shot and I almost took a bullet to the head."

Mac shook his head. "We're heading into the settlement.

There are too many innocent folks there to risk gunfire. I don't want to see anyone else get hurt."

"Enoch doesn't care who he hurts."

"Yeah, well, Enoch's not the pack leader, is he?"

Blue smiled. "No sir, he is not. And he's not gonna be."

"Good. Then let's go."

* * *

LUC SLUNK around the back side of the cabin, sniffing at the windows and its foundation. He sneezed and shook his head. The whole place reeked of omega. Even worse, it stank of *Fuller*. Why did Blue bring Fuller up here? How did they get to be such good fucking friends? Blue was supposed to be an Alpha One, but he acted like a stinking omega instead.

How had it come to this? Just a week ago, Luc was pack leader, king of his domain. He had plenty of money, first choice of food, a nice, spacious cabin, and the best of everything. Everyone in the pack waited on him hand and paw, ready to jump to obey him. Now look at him. Forced to live as a wolf to survive. His solo hunting skills were rusty too—the Alpha Ones had always hunted as a pack. Now, he didn't always catch what he stalked. Last night, he'd gone to sleep hungry.

And all because McKenna Fuller had come back to Wolf Valley.

Not for the first time, Luc cursed his father for not killing Mac outright all those years ago. If Gray Alden had not allowed Mac to live, then Luc would still be leader. He'd be sitting in front of a nice cozy fire right now, drinking moonshine and counting his money. He certainly wouldn't have to feel the shame that folks found out an omega got the best of him fifteen years ago, and again yesterday.

A growl rumbled low in his throat as he padded around

the side of the cabin. At the sound of a door opening, he froze and hunkered down in the shadows.

Mac and Blue stepped outside. It took all of Luc's self-control to keep from attacking them outright. He had to exercise patience. He knew they were wounded, but he needed to wait until the right moment to attack. He wouldn't lose them like he'd lost that jackrabbit earlier that day.

He'd been sure he had it, had stalked the damn thing for nearly fifteen minutes, but when he dashed forward intending to clamp his jaws down on the rabbit's neck, he tasted nothing but air. Something had warned the rabbit— the snap of a twig or the scent of wolf—and it had bolted a second before Luc's jaws snapped shut.

The same thing would not happen with Mac and Blue. He'd heard what Enoch had said about Blue and Mac being queer together. Oh, if only it were true! If the Alpha Ones found out, they'd back Luc without a second thought. How he would make Blue and Mac suffer before he killed them! The possibilities were endless, and every one gave him joy. He could kill one and make the other watch. Or force them to kill each other! How satisfying would that be? A fight to the death, the victor claiming only a bullet to the head as his reward.

Very, that's how satisfying.

He stayed in the shadows as Blue and Mac headed down the mountain toward the settlement, torn between following them and running to find JJ or Will and the rest of the Alpha Ones. One paw scratched at the dirt, and he took a couple of hesitant steps after them before he made up his mind.

Turning, he sprinted between the houses, weaving between the rows, making his way to the alpha cabins. He ran up onto the stoop of the third one in the second row and shifted. Naked, he shivered as he pounded on the door.

It flung open, and JJ stood framed in the open jamb. "Who

the fuck is banging on my door... Holy shit! Luc? What are you doing here?"

Luc didn't bother answering. He pushed past JJ into the cabin and went straight to the table where a half-eaten plate of beans and ham hocks sat cooling. He grabbed a blanket from a rocking chair, wrapped it around his shoulders, and then plopped in the only chair, picked up a spoon, and shoveled the food into his mouth as fast as he could.

"Jeez, help yourself, Luc."

Luc rattled an empty tin cup placed next to the plate. "Got any 'shine?"

"Nah."

"Coffee, then."

"I ain't got none of that, neither."

"Well, what the fuck *do* you have?"

JJ pointed at a metal pitcher sitting on the table. "Water. Now, you want to tell me what you're doing here, Luc?"

"What do you mean? Where else would I go?"

"I don't know. You're the one who fucking ran off instead of fighting. Man, I never took you for a coward, Luc."

In a flash, Luc shifted and jumped at JJ, knocking him to the ground. His front paws pinned JJ in place while a vicious snarl curled his lip and bared his teeth. Coward! Who was JJ to call him yellow?

"I'm sorry! I'm sorry!" JJ shifted into his wolf-self and whined.

Luc snapped at the air a couple of times to assert himself, then shifted back. "I'm no coward. It was all Mac and Blue's fault. You were there. Didn't you see them set me up?"

JJ shifted back as well and rubbed his shoulder. "Yeah, sure, Luc. I saw it. It's just that some people didn't. They think you ran."

"Well, they're wrong." Luc tipped the pitcher and scowled

at the contents. "Water? How come you don't have anything else?"

"Enoch ain't as generous as you were, I guess. I'm flat broke, and I went through my rations already. Don't get more until day after tomorrow. You're eating the last of my beans."

"Enoch! Enoch Standish? What's he got to do with anything?"

JJ smirked. "I forget you ain't been around. After Mac took up the staff and you...er, left, Enoch went into your cabin. I think he must've taken all your money. When I went in there, the safe was open and empty. He's been doling out a few bucks here and there, trying to buy people's loyalty. I told him to suck my dick—I ain't working for no Standish, not after Blue took up with Mac."

Luc felt hot anger bubble in his gut, and he lost his appetite. "He stole my money? All of it?"

"I guess so. Like I said, the safe was empty."

"What is he trying to get people to back him for?"

"I think he wants to challenge Mac for leadership."

"That old fart? He'd never last against Mac."

JJ shrugged. "Not in a fair fight, no, but I don't think Enoch fights fair."

Luc sat back, thinking. He picked up the spoon and scraped the last of the beans up. Sticking it in his mouth, he chewed and swallowed, then dropped the spoon down on the plate, where it clattered musically. "Okay, Enoch wants to go up against Mac? Fine. Let him. If he wins, Mac will be dead, and one less headache for me. If Enoch fails, even if he survives, he'll be demoted to an omega along with all the other Standishes."

"How do you figure? Mac didn't demote anybody after he won—"

Luc snarled. "After he *what?*"

"Um, after he *stole* the leadership from you."

"Damn straight. Anyway, it don't matter what Mac does. The thing is, Enoch can kill Mac, or Mac can kill Enoch. It don't matter. I'm gonna kill whoever's left standing. So, either way, I'm going to be leader again." He belched and pushed away from the table. "Come on. Let's go over to Will's. Maybe he's got some fucking 'shine. I feel the need to get a drunk on."

CHAPTER 15

"**M**cKenna Fuller is dead."

Enoch stood before the fireplace in Argyle's cabin, warming his hands in front of the fire. Irvina handed him a glass of wine, and he sipped at it. It was the good stuff, brought up from the human city. He nodded his approval. "But I have some really bad news. It's going to be hard to hear and even tougher to believe. Irvina, maybe you should take the children outside."

"For heaven's sake, Enoch, what is it?" Irvina paled and pressed a hand over her heart. "Is it Blue? Has something happened to our boy?"

He sat down and tried to compose his features into a mask of anguish. "Yes. I'm afraid so. He's dead, too, Irvina."

"No!" Irvina screamed. Her legs seemed to melt from under her, and she slumped to the floor. Enoch stood and watched her go down, sipping his wine. "No, it can't be! Not our boy. Not my Blue."

Argyle jumped up and helped Irvina to her feet. He held her, patting her back, as she sobbed. "There, there." He angled a look at Enoch. "Is it true? Did you…see him?"

147

"I'm afraid so. He's gone."

Irvina wailed anew, a piercing sound that hurt his ears. It was all Enoch could do not to smash his wineglass into her face to get her to shut up. "It's not a pretty story, Argyle. Definitely not for children's ears."

Argyle nodded. "Take the children and go to your mother's, Irvina. Go on, now."

She shakily gathered her brood and herded them out the door, weeping and bawling all the while.

Enoch drained the rest of his wine. *Really, women get so overemotional. It's pathetic. It isn't as if she doesn't have other children. What's one more or less?* He waited until they gone before speaking again. "There's more to story, like I said, and you're not going to like it."

"What is it? Tell me, Enoch. I have to know."

"Blue was a faggot, Argyle."

"What?" Argyle blinked at him, tears following the creases in his face. "You...you shut your fucking mouth, Enoch! Talking that way about my son when he's...he's..."

"Dead? Yeah, well, that don't change the truth. You really didn't know? Didn't see any signs?" Enoch shook his head. "Guess he had us all fooled. The sad truth is your boy was a fairy, and more than that, he was queer for an omega. That McKenna, the one that scared off Luc Alden and took the leadership staff."

"No. No, I don't believe it!"

"Well, it's true. Blue must've been ashamed though. I mean, you can understand why. Bad enough to be queer, but to take up with an *omega*? How low can you get?" Enoch got up and strode over to the table. He helped himself to another glass of wine. "It got to him in the end, I suppose. We found them up on the eastside of the mountain near Malcolm Ravine. Must've had an argument. He shot Mac and threw the body into the gorge. Then he killed himself, Argyle."

Argyle sank down onto his chair and covered his face with his hands. His shoulders shook as he sobbed.

"Aw, get a hold of yourself. We got bigger problems to worry on right now than a couple of dead queers."

"Blue was my son!"

"Yeah, but you got three more, and none of them is perverted. Now, listen, we got bigger worries. With Mac dead, there ain't no pack leader. Nobody knows it yet, but once word gets out, it'll be a free for all. Every man in the settlement will be making a grab for it."

"I don't care."

"Well, you *should* care. For the family, for the pack, if not for yourself. After the Aldens, the Standish clan has the highest status. I aim for it to stay that way. I'm going to be the next leader, and I need you and your boys to stand with me."

"You?" Argyle sniffed and cast a wet, baleful stare at Enoch. "What makes you think you could be leader?"

"Why not? I'm an alpha, ain't I? I got money, too, and I own a piece of the timber company. And if not me, then who? That twisted fuck Bradford? Or maybe one of the Tinkers? They spend so much time drinking their own 'shine, they can't hardly walk most days."

"M-maybe the next leader won't be an alpha. Mac was an omega. Maybe a delta or a gamma will take it this time."

Enoch growled and pitched his glass against the wall. It shattered, spraying the floor with wine and glass shards. "Goddamn it, Argyle! That's exactly the thing I'm trying to keep from happening. We got to remind these people of the way things work in this pack. They're all getting so damn uppity—before long, they'll be thinking they're as good as we are. What then? Let 'em marry our daughters and move into our cabins? Think they'll want to work logging for what we're paying them now?" He took in a long, shaky breath, trying to calm himself. Then he cast a cagey gaze at Argyle. "Besides, look what happened when an omega became leader. First off, your son ends up dead."

Argyle looked up at him, his face wet and his expression distraught. "It's what killed him. The omega. That's what happened, isn't it? My Blue was a good boy, a good man. He wasn't queer. It was the omega done it. Must've forced himself on my boy."

"Of course, of course, that's what happened. Made poor Blue so ashamed he done the only thing he could."

"Mac Fuller might as well have pulled the trigger."

Enoch nodded and bit back a smile. "Absolutely. And that's why we need to put things back the way they were, the way nature intended. So's this don't happen to no one else's boy."

Argyle seemed to sit up straighter, and his expression turned stony. "All right, Enoch. Me and the boys will back you."

A grin spread across Enoch's face. "That a boy, Argyle. You won't regret it."

"There's something I want though." Argyle grabbed Enoch's arm before Enoch could leave. "I want Blue's body brought down from the mountain. I want to give him a proper send off. And you're gonna swear to never speak of him being queer again. I don't want nobody thinking of him that way."

"Oh, sure, sure. Absolutely." Enoch pulled away from Argyle. "You get the boys and meet me at Luc Alden's cabin. We'll send word for folks to gather, and I'll give 'em the news about Blue and Fuller's deaths, then claim leadership."

Argyle's face bleached pale. "You swear you ain't gonna tell 'em about—"

"I just said I wouldn't, didn't I? Besides, folks might think there's something wrong with the Standish clan if they knew about Blue. Don't you worry—I'll blame everything on Fuller. Tell folks he went crazy and killed Blue."

"Sure, sure. Folks'll believe that. Mac is an omega. Everybody knows most of 'em ain't right in the head to begin with."

"That's right. Now, go on and get the boys. Ain't got the time to grieve right now, Argyle. We got to get control and set things to right. We got the whole pack to think of—we can't think of just ourselves right now." Enoch patted Argyle on the shoulder and then left the cabin.

Once the cabin door closed behind him, Enoch allowed himself a brief, wide smile. That'd gone easier than he'd ever believed it would. He'd been afraid Argyle would be so overcome with grief that he'd be useless, a sobbing mess. Or that Argyle would go into a blind rage and run off to extract vengeance on the Fuller clan for Blue's death. Enoch was sure Argyle believed Blue killed himself, although he thought Mac forced Blue's hand. He certainly didn't suspect Enoch was behind it. In Argyle's mind, Mac had killed Blue, pure and simple, which was fine by Enoch. In any case, Enoch's path to the leadership staff was clear.

After all, there was no one left alive for him to challenge for it. Luc ran off and hadn't been seen since. Mac was dead. Blue was dead. All Enoch had to do was publicly claim leadership, and it was as good as his.

Since the Standish family owned the timber operation for which so many deltas and gammas worked to earn enough money to see them through the harsh winter months, it stood to reason there would be few who would dare stand against him, especially with Argyle and the boys standing with him.

It was perfect.

He strolled along in a better mood than he'd enjoyed in a while. Everything was coming together. After all these years of kowtowing to the fucking Alden clan, pack leadership was finally within his grasp. It was all he could do to maintain a somber expression and not whistle a happy tune as he made his way to the Alden cabin.

A few teen pups were lounging around the cabin smoking and looking bored but shooed quick enough when Enoch strode up to the porch. McKenna had never claimed the home after running Luc off, and no one else had the balls to take it over, not even the Alpha Ones.

Alpha Ones. He snorted with disdain thinking about them. *A bunch of pups with no bite behind their bark, that's all they ever were.* Once their leader had tucked tail and run, they'd proven to be no threat to anyone, least of all him.

The door was unlocked, as he'd figured it would be. Luc had been too cocky to lock his door, and it'd stood empty since the day McKenna seized pack leadership. He let himself in. Nothing seemed to have been disturbed since his last visit when he'd emptied Luc's safe.

He took a closer look at the cabin's furnishing. Most of it was good quality; a lot of it was store-bought, which was a rarity in Wolf Valley where most goods were home crafted. He picked up a crystal vase from the mantel above the fireplace, holding it up to catch the light. A prism of color danced across the floor as the setting sun's rays passed through the facets, making him smile.

The empty safe still sat on the floor in the bedroom. Other than that, there was really no indication anyone had been in the cabin since Luc left. Good. He disliked the idea that anyone might've been in there, touching his things.

And they *were* his things. He'd make sure of it as soon as Argyle and the boys showed up. Speaking of which, he was reminded of the reason he'd come to the cabin in the first place and what he was looking to find. It wasn't in plain sight, and a quick search didn't turn it up. Enoch had a brief uneasy moment wondering if McKenna had taken it down to the omega cabins, perhaps hiding it somewhere in his family's hovel. Something told him to look more thoroughly in Luc's cabin—McKenna hadn't been seen with it since taking the leadership from Luc.

It must be here! He's probably hidden it.

Then, just as Enoch was about to give up the search and head down to the omega cabins, he found it. It'd been wedged behind a row of neatly hung clothing at the back of a handsomely carved, walnut wardrobe in the bedroom.

The leadership staff.

He hefted it and held it at arm's length. He'd thought it would be much heavier than it was. How interesting that something weighing so little carried such power. His fingers skimmed over the carved wolf heads as he noted the craquelure lacing the veneer. *I wonder how old it is. How many leaders held it? Legend says it came over with the first settlers from the old country.*

As he held the staff up and admired it, his sleeve slipped down, exposing a dark smudge on his forearm. He growled softly and tugged his shirtsleeve down. Wouldn't do for anyone to see it. Not yet, anyway.

A knock at the door brought him out of his thoughts. It opened and Argyle poked his head inside. "Enoch? You ready? Most of the settlement is out here."

Enoch smiled and gripped the staff harder. "Yeah, I am. Let's go make me leader."

Still grinning, he lifted his chin and stepped outside to meet his destiny.

CHAPTER 16

When Enoch walked out of the cabin holding the leadership staff, there was a collective intake of air as the crowd gasped in shock, but then a murmur rippled through them like wind rustling in tall grass. Everyone seemed to have a question or an opinion. Enoch held the staff up over his head, calling for their attention.

"Folks, I have bad news. McKenna Fuller and Blue Standish are dead. As far as we can figure out, Blue shot Mac, then killed himself." Enoch tried to compose his features into a mask of sorrow, but he was having a hard time doing it. He just wasn't that good an actor. "Now, don't be shedding too many tears for those two. Fact of the matter is, they was queer for each other. I don't need to tell you we don't want that kind here in Wolf Valley, 'specially not as a leader. Don't mean I wanted them dead, but I ain't sorry they're gone."

The crowd mumbled, some people nodding as if they'd known all along and agreed with Enoch, but most shaking their heads in disbelief.

"How do you know they was queer?" An alpha named

Billington shouted out, pushing toward the front of the crowd.

Enoch frowned. Fie Billington was a greedy loudmouth who liked to complain about everything. Give Billington a free loaf of bread and he'd want to know why you didn't give him butter to go with it.

The problem was, Enoch didn't like answering questions in general. It would be better if everyone just accepted what he told them and kept their mouths shut. He'd see to making that a law soon enough. No questioning the leader. Sounded good to him. "Caught them doing perverted things up at Blue's cabin."

Billington pushed his point. "How come his pa never said nothing about it?"

"Well, who could blame him? A man has a fag for a son, he ain't going to go around yapping about it." Enoch caught sight of Argyle out of the corner of his eyes. Enoch's brother looked absolutely furious -- Argyle's face was a curious shade of purple. He pressed on before Billington could ask any more questions and before Argyle had a stroke right there on the front stoop. After all, he'd promised he wouldn't mention it.

Still, Argyle should understand that promises were meant to be broken. Especially when breaking them served Enoch's purpose. "With McKenna Fuller dead, the pack is in need of a new leader. Ain't nobody alive to challenge for it, so I'm claiming it."

The crowd yammered again, folks voicing their opinions on the news. He raised the staff again and spoke louder, trying to talk over them.

"As you all know, I'm a Standish alpha. I'm a direct descendant of Ethan Standish, who come over on the first boat from the old country back in 1693. Landed at Plymouth Rock just a year after the Mayflower, and helped lead the pack all the way to Appalachia, searching for a place where wolves could run free. He helped found this settlement in Wolf Valley two years later. If anybody's got a claim to leadership, it'd be me." He shook the staff. "What say you folks?"

"I say you're a lying piece of shit and ought to get his scrawny ass kicked."

Enoch's mouth popped open and he spun, searching the crowd for who'd spoken. When he saw Mac and Blue push through the crowd, his bladder suddenly went weak. "You... you were dead! I saw you lying at the bottom of the ravine!"

"Just knocked out, I guess." Mac's expression was frosty, as if his face was carved from a block of ice. There wasn't a trace of warmth or pity in it. "Not that you bothered to check. I mean, you did shoot me in the back, but it didn't kill me."

A shudder raced down Enoch's spine. He'd left Fuller lying in a ravine, and Blue on the ground with a gun trained on him. How the hell had Griff managed to fuck this up?

Blue's face looked every bit as furious as Mac's, if not more so. His gaze sizzled with animosity. "I was alive, and you damn well knew it. You're my uncle. My fucking flesh and blood! But you paid Griff to put a bullet in my head."

The crowd gasped and began chattering among themselves again. Every glance thrown in Enoch's direction suddenly seemed suspicious and hostile.

Of all the possible outcomes, Mac and Blue returning was not one Enoch had anticipated. His mind scrambled, trying to figure out a way to turn this around, to blame them for the whole mess. "They're queer, don't forget! You can't trust a word they say."

"Being gay don't make us liars." Mac's spine was as straight as a ruler, his chin held high. "Which is more than I can say for you, Enoch Standish!"

Blue looked almost as shocked as the rest of the crowd at

first, but he seemed to recover quickly and stepped up to stand next to Mac. He didn't say anything but nodded his head.

Enoch shook the leadership staff at them. "Did you hear that? They don't even deny it! See? This is what happens when you ignore tradition. This is what happens when you turn your back on the old ways. First, a filthy omega takes the leadership staff, then you find out he's a fag!"

The omegas howled at the insult, some of them shifting. It was an unprecedented reaction, and the rest of the pack was unprepared for it. Fear rippled through the upper castes as the omegas snapped and pushed forward. Omegas always kept silently to the background, as if they were part of the furniture or landscape. They didn't get angry just because an alpha insulted them. Some of the deltas and gammas shifted, too, followed by a few alphas. Whoever hadn't shifted was yelling and arguing. Soon the entire pack was in an uproar.

"We're done being treated like we was slaves!" Angus Fuller pushed his way from the back to the front of the crowd, followed by his grown sons. "We're as much a part of the pack as all of you, ain't we? Our ancestors come over on the ship right alongside of yours. What makes you all better than us?"

Enoch bared his teeth. "You hush up and get back where you belong." He addressed the other alphas, yelling to make himself heard above the din. "See? This is what comes from straying away from tradition. You think an omega would've dared speak out at a meeting like this back in the day? Not if he wanted to keep his ugly hide on his bones, he didn't!"

"Enoch, enough!" Mac's voice was deep enough and loud enough to stun everyone else into silence. He strode up toward the cabin porch. "In case you've forgotten, I'm not dead, and therefore still leader of this pack. You want the right to hold that staff? Then you'd better formally challenge me for it, or else give it over."

Argyle and his sons stepped up at a signal from Enoch. He allowed a satisfied smile to lift his lips as he flicked his fingers toward Mac. "Take him away. I have no time for lying queers."

The three men stepped off the porch and approached Mac and Blue, then turned and stared at Enoch with undisguised malice. Argyle spoke. "You lied to us. Told us my boy was dead! I don't believe a fucking word that comes out of your mouth, Enoch. You're a lying snake." He tugged Blue in for a tight hug, then shook Mac's hand.

Enoch was shocked and suddenly afraid. He could feel the mood of the crowd turning against him even more than it had been before. Now the alphas, deltas, and gammas were glaring at him in addition to the omegas. His heart thumped hard in his chest, and a cold sweat broke out across his forehead as he felt his claim on pack leadership slipping away. "Argyle! I'm your brother!"

"You're no brother of mine. Not anymore. You're dead to me, Enoch." Argyle and his other sons took up places directly behind Blue and Mac.

"Okay, Enoch. It's over." Mac's steps toward Enoch were slow but purposeful. His muscles were clearly tensed, and his expression looked like he meant business.

Enoch was at a loss. He hadn't anticipated any of this— not Mac and Blue returning from the dead, so to speak, nor Argyle's defection. He stammered, trying to talk his way out of it. "Now, Mac, see here. You don't want this staff. It's a heavy burden, son. You're young, and you've got a life outside of Wolf Valley. You don't want to tie yourself down in this pissant little village."

"That's not your decision to make." Mac stepped up onto

the porch and yanked the leadership staff out of Enoch's hand.

Enoch had no hope of holding on to the staff. He simply wasn't strong enough, either physically or, as it turned out, mentally. After letting go of it, he stepped away. "No hard feelings, right?"

"Are you insane?" Mac shook his head. "You ordered Griff to kill Blue, and you fucking shot me, yourself! That's attempted murder, Enoch. Something like that can't go unpunished. Not to mention, I don't think many folks here would feel safe with somebody like you running around free."

"W-what are you going to do?" Enoch's eyes went wide with terror, and he couldn't control the tremble in his voice or his hands.

Mac motioned to Blue. "What does the pack do with criminals? I don't think I remember a jail in the settlement."

"There was never a jail, Mac. It's always been the same as when you live here before. Somebody breaks pack law, he or she is punished, usually by being demoted to a lower caste. If it's an extreme crime, they're exiled." Blue spat at Enoch's feet. "Either one is a good choice as far as I'm concerned."

After heaving a sigh, Mac shook his head. "I'm going to have to think about it, Blue. I don't like making rash decisions of that magnitude, even when it involves a lowdown piece of shit like Enoch. Argyle, will you and the boys take Enoch and lock him up in his cabin until I decide what to do with him?"

Enoch tried to run, but Argyle and his sons caught up quickly. He sputtered and tried to struggle against the men who grabbed and held him. "You can't do this to me! I'm a direct descendant of—"

"Oh, shut the fuck up, Enoch. Everyone here, every last one of us, is a direct descendant of somebody who crossed over on that damned ship. I'm sick of hearing you. You've caused enough trouble and given us enough headaches for today." Argyle growled and pulled him away.

The crowd parted, allowing Argyle and his sons to haul Enoch away, but turned back to Mac as soon as they passed through. It didn't seem as if anyone there was sorry to see Enoch go either.

* * *

ONE PAIR of eyes watched in silence as the events played out. Hidden in the thick brush to the east of the cabin, Luc remained as his wolf-self, whose eyesight was infinitely sharper, and whose instincts were far more honed than his man-self's could ever hope to be.

He was the only one, aside from his Alpha Ones, who'd known Mac and Blue were alive, and he wasn't disappointed by that asshole Enoch's reaction when Mac and Blue strode up to the cabin. If he didn't hate both of them so intensely, he might've actually been happy they'd survived Enoch's weak plot to take over the pack.

Then again, now he had the opportunity to kill them himself, and that sort of made up for Enoch's bumbling attempt, and *did* make him happy. His tail thumped behind him as his excitement got the better of his wolf-self.

There were too many people here now, too many who might not readily back him, who might remember how he'd run away from the last fight between him and Mac.

All he had to do was wait for the opportune moment to challenge Mac and take back leadership of the pack and satisfy the bloodlust stirring within him at the same time.

CHAPTER 17

"All right, all right! Calm down, everyone, please!" Mac shouted, holding the staff up over his head, trying to quiet the crowd. He frowned and finally lowered it. While everyone wanted to be heard, nobody seemed too keen on listening. He decided to wait it out, hoping they would just naturally wind themselves down.

He felt Blue's arm press against his, and the warmth penetrated right through his shirtsleeve and brought a smile to his lips. "Hey. Pretty crazy stuff, huh?"

"You're telling me. What the fuck am I supposed to do now?" Mac glanced back at the crowd. None of the people gathered seemed to be paying him the slightest bit of attention. They were still too busy chattering and arguing amongst themselves. "I'm not cut out for this shit."

"You're doing fine. I'm proud of you, Mac."

"Gee, thanks, dad."

That earned him an elbow in the ribs. "Fucker." The word was coarse, but the smile on Blue's face belied its harshness. "You'd better try to get their attention again or we'll be here all night."

Mac sighed but nodded. He raised the staff again. "Folks! Could I have your attention, please?" His throat hurt from all the yelling. He cleared it and tried again. "Come on, now, settle down."

"Why should we listen to you? You're nothing but an omega. I think Enoch was right. What makes you good enough to lead?" An alpha whose name Mac didn't recall stepped up.

This raised the hackles on a number of omegas, who shouted out at the insult. "Ain't nothing wrong with being an omega!"

The alpha wasn't backing down easily. "He wasn't nothing when he got banished, and he come back here, tailed tucked, so that tells us he wasn't nothing out there, neither!"

"That's not true!" Blue stepped forward. Mac put his hand on Blue's arm. The last thing he wanted was for Blue to get mixed up in a free-for-all argument, but Blue shook him off. "You don't know the first thing about Mac. Gray Alden banished him when he wasn't much more than a pup, but he survived. More than that, he got himself educated and made a life for himself out there in the human world! I'll have you know Mac has more money than any of us will likely ever see in our lifetimes. He could've walked on out of here after the shitty way everyone treated him, but he didn't. He challenged Luc for leadership because it was the right thing to do for everybody, and he won it fair and square."

Blue was working himself up into a fine mood, getting red in the face and stabbing his finger at the crowd. Mac tugged his hand down. "Blue, let it go. Come on, settle down."

"No! I'm not going to stand here and let them bad mouth you anymore." He scowled at the crowd. "Did you forget Mac got shot? He did. Enoch got him right here." Blue tugged on the back of Mac's shirt despite Mac's protests and

162

exposed the bandage hiding the wound. Blood had begun to seep through it, bright red against the white. "Did he lie down and give up? Fuck no. He faced down Enoch and took back the staff. Think he did it for himself? He don't need the fucking pack... This pack needs *him*. And you all better appreciate that fact before he decides you're not worth the effort."

The crowd stared at Blue and Mac in stunned silence. Then a murmur rose as they began discussing among themselves the information about Mac Blue had just given them. Mac picked up the words *omega, rich,* and *educated* more than once.

He chewed on the inside of his cheek for a minute, fighting to corral the emotions threatening to escape his control. "Thanks, Blue."

Blue looked sheepish, and one shoulder shrugged. "Got a little carried away, but you're welcome."

The attack came out of nowhere.

A gray blur streaked in from the east, flying across the porch and hitting Mac in the side. The impact lifted him off his feet and flung him onto the ground in front of the cabin. Suddenly, he found himself fending off a snarling wolf, a furious one hundred and fifty pounds of sinewy muscle and snapping teeth.

He heard Blue's voice calling to him. "It's Luc! Get the fuck off him! No, let me go. Let me go, damn it!"

As Mac rolled, trying to push the wolf off him, he saw two men holding Blue's arms. One of them was Blue's father, Argyle. Blue was struggling, straining to break free, but his kin wouldn't let go.

Mac realized that, as far as the pack was concerned, he was being challenged for leadership. They wouldn't allow Blue to interfere or help in any way—it was Mac's fight, to be won or lost on his own. *So, even though Luc ran away when I had the upper hand the last challenge, I have to fight him all over again? Well, fuck me sideways.*

He gritted his teeth, muscles straining to keep killer jaws from snapping closed on his throat. "Listen up, Luc. This shit ends now, you hear me? No more running like a fucking coward." He heaved and rolled Luc over, his hands tight around Luc's throat.

Killing someone was not as easy as they made it seem on television and in the movies. It was hard work, especially when you had to do it with your bare hands, and they were fighting back. His hands and arms cramped as he bore down, trying to squeeze the breath from Luc's body while Luc bucked and snapped under him. Already weakened by the bullet he'd taken to the back, Mac realized he was at a distinct disadvantage. This fight required endurance his man-self didn't possess. It also demanded the savage part of his nature. He decided it was time to stop thinking like a human and start behaving like a wolf.

In the blink of an eye, he shifted into an equally gigantic, pissed-off pitch-black wolf.

Shifting had two immediate effects. First, Mac's size and strength surprised Luc, who evidently had assumed Mac's omega wolf would be slighter, more delicate than his own alpha wolf-self. He must've been sadly-- and shockingly-- disappointed because he froze—for only a heartbeat, to be sure, but long enough for Mac to see the fear in his eyes.

Second, Mac's clothing, shredded during the change, became a spider web of fabric, tangling both their paws and slowing the fight as they struggled to free themselves. Vicious snarls rent the air, bringing shouts of excitement and encouragement from the crowd.

Luc was the first to wriggle free, but Mac gained his feet a moment later. The two wolves separated and circled one another warily, growling, each feinting in to snap at the air with powerful jaws.

They met like two titans, on hind legs, front paws scrambling, muzzles dueling, biting, each one's teeth trying to score in the flesh of the other. They danced around in a tight circle, broke, then charged again.

Pained yips intermingled with the snarls and growls as teeth found purchase. Mac took a painful bite to the shoulder; in turn, he tasted blood when his jaws closed on Luc's hindquarter. Still they circled and fought, dashing in and out, jumping and weaving.

As the fight grew wilder, the circle of onlookers grew wider. The crowd backed away both to give the combatants more room to move, as well as not risk their own skins to an inadvertent bite from Luc or Mac.

Luc had nowhere to run this time. The crowd had them trapped—he would need to fight his way to the tree line, and by now, he must've known it. To his credit, Mac grudgingly admitted, Luc exhibited some guts, refusing to show his belly even though he was wounded and outmatched.

Both were panting and showing signs of tiring. Again and again they clashed, biting and scratching, paws bloodied by wounds inflicted by wicked teeth.

The coppery smell of blood tinged the air, the scent fueling Mac's rage. He was nearly beyond rational thinking now, almost fully immersed in his wolf-self. Instinct ruled his brain and edged out human reason. In his heart, without it being put into human words, he knew this fight would end with him either killing or being killed, or at the least, leading or being led, and his wolf-self had no intention of submitting to the latter in either outcome.

Luc was showing signs of fatigue. He panted heavily, sides heaving as he doggedly tried to fend off Mac's attacks, but Mac's teeth scored more and more often. It wouldn't be long now before Mac had Luc on his back, and one final snap of Mac's jaws would proclaim a victor.

"Mac! Mac, stop! You're going to kill him!"

Mac's ears twitched. The voice was human and familiar. It carried weight with him, even in his wolf-self. He shook his head and renewed his attack on Luc.

"No, Mac! Please! You're better than this. You don't need to kill him. I know you. It'll haunt you if you do!"

Again, Mac paused, distracted by the familiar voice. His man-self took the opportunity to rise up, forcing his wolf-self into submission. *What am I doing? Blue is right. I'm trying to change things in this pack. Killing Luc will only foster the old way of doing things.*

Before he could shift back into his man-self, Luc lunged. He caught Mac's neck but was too weak to keep a grip when Mac shook him off. Mac snapped in reflex, catching Luc's right foreleg. The crack of bone was audible as Mac's powerful jaws broke it.

Luc's shriek of pain began as a howl but ended as a piercing scream as he shifted. His arm was obviously broken, his bone jutting at an odd angle. Blood flowed from several bites ranging from shallow to deep. He collapsed on the ground, writhing in pain.

Mac shifted, and stood over him. It was plain Luc needed medical attention by one of the pack's healers, but Mac couldn't allow it, not until their dispute was finally settled. "Yield, Luc."

"Finish him! Finish him!" Bloodlust had infected the crowd. Leadership challenges weren't usually settled by the death of an opponent, but it wasn't unheard of, either. Luc had won the leadership staff that way. Wouldn't it be poetic justice for him to lose it the same way?

They were to be disappointed this time. Mac's glare was

enough to silence them. He returned his attention to Luc. "Yield, Luc. It's over. Say the words."

Luc whimpered and huddled on the ground, protecting his broken limb. "I…I yield." His voice was a whisper, but it was loud enough to be heard by those folks standing closest, and repeated to those too far to hear.

"Luc yielded!"

"It's over."

"Mac is still leader!"

Then another voice spoke up, and it reached into Mac's soul, calming him and setting the beast within him to rest. "I'm proud of you, Mac. You did good."

He smiled at Blue. "Only because I heard you remind me what it is I want to change about the pack." He glanced down at Luc, who was moaning in pain. "We need a healer here. Who is healer for the alphas?"

"I am, but he's no alpha. Not anymore." A grizzled old man spoke up, then turned his head and spat. "He's the omega healer's problem now."

Sylva pushed her way through the crowd and walked up to Mac. She turned and glared at the crowd, pride in the tilt of her chin. "I'm healer for the omegas, but Luc here caused nothing but heartache and harm to the omegas as leader. Still, the new leader," she said, and cast an incredulous look up at Mac, "has decided Luc won't die or be banished for his crimes. So, I'll help Luc, not because he lost the challenge and his former standing within the pack, but because he is *of* the pack and injured. Even though I still think he's a piece of shit."

Mac chuckled and placed a hand on her shoulder. "Well said, and thank you, Ma."

"Yeah, well. You're the leader, not me. If it was up to me, the little bastard would be dead.

She looked hard at him and cocked her head. "You need healing, too, Mac."

"Not as badly as he does, Ma. I'll come down to see you in a little while."

She nodded and motioned for a couple of men to help carry Luc to her cabin. They hefted him up and left, heading toward the omega cabins.

"I can heal you, Mac. You're an alpha now." The same grizzled old man stepped up, smiling. "Like I said, I'm healer for the alphas. Makes me chief healer for the pack, I reckon."

Mac snarled at him, and the man backed up a few steps, eyes wide with fear. "You won't touch me. My ma is now chief healer of this pack."

The man stammered. "W-hat? Why? Because she's your ma? She's still just an omega—"

"No, not because we're related-- because she was willing to help a pack mate when you wouldn't touch him, and as far as I'm concerned, that's the sign of a good healer."

Mac turned his most heated gaze on the crowd, meeting as many eyes as possible. "For the last time, are there any here who challenge my right to lead?"

Waiting, watching, Mac felt tension tearing at his already bone-weary and aching body. His wounds still bled; every muscle felt sore. He wanted to go home with Blue to the little cabin up by the logging camp, soak in a nice warm bath, and then fuck Blue until the pain went away, but knew he couldn't. Not yet, anyway.

Minutes ticked by as he waited. He wanted, *needed* to be sure.

No one answered his challenge. Everyone stood still, staring back him, but not in hostility—at least, not all of them. It was apparent some were not pleased an omega had rightfully and completely taken leadership of the pack, but most faces held benign expressions. They were waiting for him to give orders, to tell them what to do.

Blue handed him the leadership staff, and Mac thrust it into the air, holding it in both hands over his head despite the pain it caused him. Applause and hoots of celebration from the omegas drowned out the far more lackluster welcome from the others.

All good things in time, he thought. *They'll come around. They'd better.*

Finally, he nodded. "All right then. The first and only order of business for the rest of today-- go home. Eat. Rest. Hug your kids. Tomorrow starts a new day and a new life for this pack."

Mac slung an arm over Blue's shoulder and tugged him in, placing a kiss on his forehead. If there was any doubt in the truth of Enoch's accusations of Mac and Blue's sexual identities, there was none now.

And he couldn't care less.

Like he said, tomorrow was going to start a whole new chapter in the life of the pack, and the first rule he was going to institute was going to be "live and let live."

CHAPTER 18

Mac limped out of his parents' cabin with a poultice strapped to his chest that reeked of onion and matched the one on his back, and over two dozen stitches. Still, Sylva promised he would heal practically as good as new. Maybe he'd have a few new scars, but Blue thought they would make him even sexier.

Luc had fared far worse in the fight. He lay unconscious on a blanket in a corner of Sylva's cabin, covered in reeking poultices and bandages. His right arm was set in a birch bark cast, but his fingers were swollen up like sausages. Luc's face was a mess too. There was a bite mark on his cheek, and both eyes were nearly swollen shut. It was almost enough to make Blue feel sorry for him.

Almost, but not quite.

They'd gone up to Blue's cabin after that, even though the hike tired Mac out. When they got inside, Blue twisted his fingers into the fabric of Mac's shirt and pulled him in close. The kiss he planted on Mac's full lips was deep, wet, and hungry. His body hardened, and he rubbed himself wantonly against Mac's meaty thigh.

"I want, Mac. Bad."

Mac moaned against Blue's cheek, the scruff on his jaw scraping Blue's skin. "Me too." Then he inexplicably pulled away. "But we can't. Not yet."

Blue had been leaning against Mac and almost fell over. He recovered his balance and tried to make the feat look less awkward than it felt. "Why the fuck not?"

"First of all, I'm fucking exhausted. I feel like somebody beat me with a rock and hung me out wet." Mac walked over to the bed and carefully lowered himself onto the mattress. His eyes closed, and for a minute, Blue thought he'd drifted off to sleep. "Besides, I've got no time. I need to think, Blue. There are details I need to get straight in my head before I call a meeting."

"What meeting?"

"The meeting I'm going to call tomorrow."

Blue rolled his eyes. "I get *that* part. What's this meeting going to be about?"

Mac cracked an eye open and looked at him. "The future of this pack. I wasn't lying after the fight, Blue. I'm going to make some big changes, and not everyone is going to like them. I can't hold off too long before talking to everyone." He sucked in a breath and hissed it out between his teeth. "I'm sorry, hon."

Blue sighed, then walked over to the bed and removed Mac's boots. He put them on the floor next to the bed, then pulled the quilt up over Mac's body. "Don't be. I understand. Look at you. You're so bruised up right now if you think too hard you'll give yourself a nosebleed. I can wait, the meeting can wait, and so can the pack. You're not going to do anything about it today, anyway."

"No, it *can't* wait."

Blue frowned down at him. "You listen to me, McKenna Fuller. You may be leader, but I'm not about to let you fall over dead because you pushed yourself too hard. Take a nap, at least. While you're dozing, I'll brew up some of that tea your ma made for your pain and warm up the plate of food she sent with us. Then, after we eat, you can worry on these changes you want to make."

From the soft snores coming from Mac, he realized he was talking to himself. Mac had already fallen fast asleep. He smiled and bent down to place a gentle kiss on Mac's forehead. "I get the feeling life ain't gonna ever be the same while I'm around you, McKenna Fuller. And you know what? It may be a little scary sometimes, but it sure as fuck ain't gonna be dull."

* * *

IT TURNED out Mac found the time and energy to love on Blue after all.

A dozen and a half times, in fact.

Almost a week passed before he could walk relatively pain free, and a full ten days had gone by before his ma would consent to remove the stitches. During Mac's downtime, he and Blue had managed to set the mattress to rockin' at least once a day, and sometimes twice. Of course, in the beginning, Blue had to do all the work, but still, Mac hadn't heard any complaints from Blue on the subject.

Now nearly two weeks had gone by since the fight, and while he'd been recuperating, in addition to bumping uglies with Blue, he did a lot of thinking. He managed to outline a plan for the pack's future, but more than that, an idea occurred to him that might just explain the constant underlying hostility among his people. If he was right, it wouldn't be an easy fix. He planned to go down to the human city to research the possibility, not mentioning it to anyone until he was sure. That would come a little later. For now, he'd present his vision for the future of the pack in an open meeting he called on the first day he actually started feeling more like his old self.

One pressing matter he did have to attend to during his convalescence was the matter of Enoch Standish. They'd had Enoch locked up in the Standish cabin's small root cellar since the day of the fight, and according to Blue's father, Argyle, Enoch spent every minute of it whining, crying, complaining, cursing, and pretty much driving the rest of the Standish clan half crazy. Argyle had come to Blue's cabin in desperation, asking for help.

"Please. We haven't slept a wink since the fight. He keeps us up all hours, banging on the door, throwing things around, screaming and yelling. Blue, your ma is having fits over it. He wakes the pups up and they start bawling... At this point, I don't care if it's Enoch or me, but somebody's gotta go."

Blue shrugged and turned to Mac. "What do you think, Oh Grand and Glorious Leader? What do you want to do about Enoch?"

Mac sighed and lay back against his pillow. "Oh, man, I almost forgot all about him."

Argyle clucked his tongue. "Well, if you'd killed him then, like I said, he wouldn't be taxing you now."

Mac shook his head. "No, the killing has to stop. Banishing him might work, I suppose, but what's to keep him from coming back again like I did?"

"This is a different situation, Mac." Argyle stroked his beard as if considering the matter. "You were just a kid when Gray Alden sent you away. You didn't deserve to be banished, and I think everybody knew it. When you come back, your kin took you in, gave you a place to stay. Nobody's stupid enough to take Enoch back. He done burnt all his bridges."

Argyle made sense, but Mac was still uncomfortable.

Banishment could be the equivalent of a death sentence if the person was too young or too old to survive on their own. It was only sheer luck he'd made it. He had doubts Enoch, who was getting on in years and already weakened, would be as fortunate.

He pondered on it for a full day and night before he finally came up with what he thought was a fair solution to his problem. When it came to him, it seemed so simple he was surprised he hadn't thought of it sooner.

Rather than hike down to the settlement and possibly reinjure himself, he'd sent word to have Enoch brought up to Blue's cabin. The sun was past its zenith when the small contingent consisting of Blue's brothers and Argyle led Enoch, wrists bound behind his back, up the mountainside.

Mac sat on a rocker on the cabin's porch. It was his first time outside since the fight, and he was enjoying the feel of cool, fresh mountain air on his face when he saw the men coming up the path from the logging camp. The leadership staff leaned against the cabin beside his chair.

"Blue? They're here."

Blue came outside and stood next to Mac. "Now, you remember what you promised. You sit, and you don't get yourself all worked up. You take care of business; then you're right back in bed, right?"

"Yes, mama."

He got a gentle nudge from Blue for his sarcasm. "Shut up or I'll tell your real ma."

"Tattletale." He smiled up at Blue, then quickly composed his features into a stern poker face and waited in silence for the men to walk up to the porch.

He gave Argyle and the Standish boys a brief nod. "Argyle, boys. Good to see you. Thank you for dragging his sorry ass all the way up here."

"Our pleasure, Alpha. It's about time something got done with him. He's been driving all of us out of our ever-lovin' minds." Argyle pushed Enoch to the front and center, standing directly behind Enoch to prevent any attempt at escape.

"Well, ain't you just the king shit? Sitting on your throne up there, waiting to pass judgment on your betters." Enoch spat at Mac, although he had no momentum and his spittle landed in the dirt only a foot in front of him. A thin line of drool snaked from his lower lip. "Disgusting. That's what it is."

"Enoch, you're not making things better for yourself talking like this. Don't you ever learn?" Blue shook his head. "I swear, you must be the dumbest man alive."

"How dare you call yourself a Standish!" Enoch snarled at him. "I am a direct descendant of—"

Blue, Argyle, and Blue's brothers finished the sentence in harmony. "...Ethan Standish, who came over on the first boat from the old country back in 1693." Blue rolled his eyes. "We know, we know. We've only heard about a bajillion times. It means nothing. Now, shut up and listen."

"Enoch, your crimes against members of this pack, myself included, are worthy of a death sentence. You stole money that rightfully belonged to the pack. You shot me, tried to kill me, then ordered one of your men to put a bullet in Blue's head." Mac stood up, setting his jaw against the pain, but not feeling right about passing judgment while sitting down. He glared at Enoch. In his peripheral vision, he could see Argyle and the others watching him carefully, as if waiting to see if an omega could truly pass judgment on an alpha.

Well, he could, and he would. Just not in the way they'd imagined.

"Thinking Blue and I were dead, you tried to seize the

leadership staff for yourself without having to prove yourself worthy by challenging me for it, as is pack law. These crimes are unforgiveable, and the punishment must fit the severity of them. Yet, should I declare you an omega, you've proven so deceitful you can't be trusted to live among us, but you can't be trusted to stay away if I were to banish you, either."

His words seemed to leave only one other option -- a death sentence -- and Enoch's face paled visibly as the realization seemed to sink in. His legs wobbled, and soon enough Argyle and the boys were supporting his weight to keep him from falling down, rather than running.

"But I don't believe killing you would make life any better for anyone else, other than ridding the pack of an annoyance. Enoch, you're the product of your generation, and every generation that came before you. You were raised in an elitist belief system serving the few by breaking the backs of the many. I don't know if you're even *capable* of change anymore, nor do I have the patience or inclination to try to get you to change your mind. Now--"

Argyle interrupted, looking confused. "If you ain't gonna kill him, what are you gonna do with him?"

Mac scowled at Argyle. "I'm getting to that." He lifted the leadership staff and tapped the ground with it three times. "Enoch, you are banished from the sight of this pack forever. You will never set foot on pack land again, or see the faces of those who once considered you kin. As soon as I'm healed enough to travel, Blue and I, along with Argyle and his boys will escort you off the mountain and down to the human city. There I will sign you into the Mt. Hope Nursing Facility. You will remain there, living as a human, for the rest of your days. I--"

Argyle cut in again, earning himself another fierce look from Mac. "Don't them places cost money? The pack ain't gonna want to spend another red nickel on Enoch."

"Interrupt me again, Argyle, and I may put you two in adjoining rooms." He could hear Blue stifle a chuckle, but ignored it. "As I was saying, *I* will pay for your expenses, not the pack. You've caused the pack enough misfortune; I won't add to it by making them pay for your keep."

It seemed Argyle could be taught. He waited until Mac finished speaking before asking another question. "Why? Why spare his life at all? Wouldn't it be easier and cheaper to just kill his sorry ass?"

"Yes, it would, but that's not the point. Money isn't an issue -- I have plenty. It's more because I believe violence just begets violence and doesn't really contribute anything except the need for more brutality. We have to learn to temper the aggressive instincts of our wolf-selves with the progressive and compassionate thinking of our man-selves. We must evolve, and I think this sentence for Enoch is a step in the right direction."

Argyle still wasn't satisfied, but Mac was fine with his reluctance. Concerns should be voiced; decisions should be questioned. "What if he shifts in this home you want to put him in?"

Mac looked down at Enoch and sadly shook his head. "He can't shift. Not anymore. Right, Enoch?"

The men gasped and stared at Enoch in horror. None of them could imagine a worse fate than not being able to access their wolf-selves.

Enoch grimaced, and the last fight seemed to leach out of him. "How did you figure it out?"

"When I confronted you for the leadership staff, I realized you hadn't shifted. Not when I grabbed the staff and not when I ordered you taken away. I even had you locked up in the cabin instead of the root cellar as a test, and you failed it. You see, you never shifted to try to escape. The door of the cabin was locked, but if you shifted you could've gone out

177

the window and run into the forest. Anyone else would've done it or at least tried to. That's when I realized you couldn't shift anymore."

"Is that true, Enoch? You can't shift?" Blue looked astounded. "I didn't think it was possible."

"Oh, it's possible, sure." Argyle answered for Enoch, who remained silent, staring at the ground. "There are diseases that can keep a man from shifting. The worst is the Black Mark." He took Enoch's arm and pushed up the sleeve. A dark, malignant-looking mark smudged the skin just below Enoch's elbow. "How long you had this thing, Enoch?"

Enoch pulled his arm away and covered the mark with his sleeve. He looked as defeated as a man could get. "Long enough. A couple of years now, I reckon."

"That's why you wanted the leadership staff, isn't it?"

"It ain't fair!" Enoch looked from Blue to Argyle to the boys and back again, but he avoided Mac. "What good's an alpha that can't shift? An alpha without his wolf-self is useless. He's worse than an omega!"

"So, you thought stealing the leadership would replace the status you thought you were losing." Mac sighed. "Twisted thinking, but understandable to a point, I guess. What you've done just proves what I've been saying all along -- a man's worth shouldn't be determined by his birth, but by his deeds." He signaled to Argyle and the boys. "Take him back to the cabin and lock him up. Make sure he's fed -- he looks skinny -- and get my ma to take a look at him. There's nothing she can do about the Black Mark, but it can't hurt for her to give him the once-over."

Blue nudged Mac as they watched Argyle and the boys lead Enoch toward the logging camp and the settlement beyond. "Won't the humans wonder when they see it? The mark, I mean."

"I've seen marks like that before, Blue, on humans. They suffer from it too. If I'm right, and I think I am, they call it melanoma. Skin cancer."

CHAPTER 19

Almost everyone showed up in front of the alpha leader's cabin for Mac's first official pack meeting. The only ones missing were those too ill to come or those too young, and of course, Luc, who was still too injured to walk, and who no one wanted to see anyway.

They'd taken Enoch down to the human city just a few days before as soon as Mac was healed enough to make the trip. Argyle gave proof he was next of kin and signed Enoch into the nursing facility. Mac made arrangements for the monthly payment for Enoch's upkeep.

Enoch had wailed and raged, lashing out at everyone within reach. He became so violently out of control the doctors had to sedate him. Mac was sure they'd test Enoch and determine he suffered from early dementia as well as from skin cancer. Certainly, no human would believe the old man's tales of shapeshifting wolves. He knew they'd have no reason to test Enoch's DNA, which he thought would be the only way to prove Enoch wasn't entirely human. Even if they did, he was confident the doctors would write any anomalies off as test contamination.

After they had their business with Enoch settled, Mac sent Argyle back to the pack. He and Blue needed to stay in town for a few days more. All he told Argyle was that he, Mac, had business that needed attending. Argyle, conditioned to obey the Alpha, didn't question what that business was, not that Mac would've told him if he did.

They got a room in the best hotel in town -- which wasn't saying much. It wasn't the Ritz, but it was clean and had both a jacuzzi tub and room service. As soon as they were settled, Mac made a long-distance telephone call to Blaine Taylor in California.

"Mac! Good to hear from you. How are you? Where are you? Are you in town?" Blaine sounded far too happy to hear from him, and he could hear Blue growling softly. Blue's lupine hearing could pick up every word Blaine said. Mac smiled and shushed Blue.

"Hello, Blaine. No, sorry. I'm not in California. I'm calling about the email you sent me a while back. About the company you work for that's interested in mining my neck of the Appalachians?"

"Yes, yes. Of course, I remember." The business tone of Mac's voice leached some of the excitement out of Blaine's voice.

"What exactly is your company looking to find? We already know there's no coal, oil, or natural gas on the mountain. No gold, either."

"Silver, Mac. We have reason to believe that mountain has rich silver veins running through it."

Mac gave Blue a knowing look. It was exactly what he'd suspected. The pack was literally sitting on top of a silver deposit, and had been for generations. Silver -- the one metal to which every pack, not just theirs, carried a genetic sensitivity.

For generations, the silver in the earth had been

poisoning the pack, affecting them mentally, causing irrational behavior, anger, and violence. Because of the silver, they'd become hostile to each other, and each new generation was worse than the one before it.

"Holy shit!" Blue gasped. His face was pale as the implications of what he'd heard sunk in. "What are we going to do, Mac?"

Mac motioned for him to quiet down. "Blaine, suppose I wanted to work out a deal with your company to mine the silver. But in return, I need a favor. I need your company's assurance that Wolf Valley, in particular the land bordering Jewel Creek, will be mined first. Can that be done?"

"I'll need to talk to my people and get back to you on it. I think it can be arranged though."

"Excellent. Leave a message on my cell. We'll take it from there. Thanks, Blaine. Bye." He hung up, and turned to Blue.

"What the hell just happened?" Blue pointed at the phone. "Who was that guy?"

"A friend from the past. Blaine is scientist I know who works for Cal Tech. He's also an advisor for a mining company. Don't you get it? There's silver in the mountain, Blue! That's what's made our pack so crazy. Some of us are more susceptible to silver poisoning, I guess, like Enoch and Luc, and Gray before them, but we're all affected to a degree."

"So, what do we do about it?"

Mac smiled "We move." He put a hand up when Blue opened his mouth to argue. "Just temporarily. It has to be done. We can't stay and continue to let the pack be poisoned. Once the silver is mined out, we can return. Until then, I'll find us a nice little empty town for sale -- believe it or not there are plenty of them -- and see about buying it for the pack."

"People aren't going to like this, Mac."

"They're just going to have to deal, Blue. I'm leader, and what I say goes, right?"

Blue shook his head. "You're crazy. Not silver-crazy, just plain, ordinary, everyday crazy. But you know what? I love that about you. Now kiss me and get me in that tub. I want wet, slippery, soapy sex."

* * *

ONCE THEY WERE BACK HOME at the mountain cabin, Mac needed to attend to his other duties as leader, and Luc was his number-one concern. Mac was going to have to decide what to do about him, and it was a much thornier problem than the one Mac had faced with Enoch. Luc was younger than Enoch by decades and, once recovered, would be much healthier and stronger. Shifting was not a problem for Luc, who was also more intelligent, craftier, and meaner, had a vindictive streak a mile wide, and couldn't be trusted as far as Mac could toss him. He'd never stay away if Mac banished him, but couldn't be locked up in a facility like Enoch either.

Worst of all, he couldn't expect to reason with Luc. Luc would want vengeance on Mac to try to recoup what Luc would no doubt see as his lost honor. The situation had the potential to get ugly.

Still, Luc was a problem Mac didn't need to deal with just yet, since Luc wouldn't be able to go anywhere for a while. Mac hadn't realized how badly he'd damaged Luc in their fight. The broken arm was the least of Luc's troubles—Mac had inflicted some serious internal injuries as well. Sylva was confident Luc would survive, but it would take time for him to heal, and there was a chance he would never mend completely.

They'd brought the wooden kitchen table out from the

cabin and placed it on the porch. Mac, Blue, and Argyle sat behind it, looking out at the pack who'd gathered there.

"You really rich?" A gamma named Cooper stepped forward. His wife and two small children stayed close behind him. "Blue says you're a millionaire. That true?"

Mac nodded at the man. "My net worth is closer to a hundred million because I've invested well, but the money doesn't matter. What a man has in his bank account doesn't make him a good leader. Look at Enoch. Look at Luc. They both had money, but neither one put the good of the pack ahead of his own selfish needs. Both of them just wanted the power."

Cooper didn't seem entirely satisfied with Mac's answer. "Yeah, that's what most rich people say, ain't it? The money never matters 'cept to them that don't have any."

"I will make you a pledge here and now, Cooper. From this day forward, this pack will always provide equally for all its members. No one will go hungry or without, not anymore."

"We've all heard promises like that before. What makes you so different from Luc or Gray or the others then?"

He stood up and placed his hands on the table before him, bracing his weight on his arms. "Well, for one thing, I don't *want* to be leader."

That set the crowd muttering angrily all over again.

. "Don't want to be leader? Didn't he just fight nearly to the death for the staff?"

"What does he mean?"

"He nearly killed Luc to be leader!"

"If he didn't want it, why didn't he let Enoch have it?"

"The pack needs a leader. If not him, then who?"

It was several long minutes before Mac managed to wrangle their attention and quiet them down again. "What I mean is that I'm not sure this pack needs a *single* leader anymore. It hasn't worked very well for anyone in recent years--"

"We've *always* had a leader!" Cooper shook off his wife's restraining hand and took a step forward. It was a daring move for someone who wasn't an alpha, and Mac was simultaneously impressed and annoyed. "Who's gonna protect us? Who's gonna make sure we all got food and shelter now that winter's coming on? Who's gonna keep the alphas from taking what little the rest of us got?"

Cooper's words set the pack to arguing again, their voices growing louder as their fear and uncertainty rose. What started as a low buzz soon grew into vocal thunder strained with barely repressed panic. The alphas were incensed that a gamma would dare impugn their intentions, his close-kin stood with Cooper, and the rest were afraid of retribution by the higher-ranked members.

Mac roared loudly enough to make Cooper back right up to where he'd been before and stunned the rest into silence. "Will you shut up and listen!" He took a breath and reached for patience he wasn't sure he still had. Incredibly, he found some. "I didn't say the pack *wouldn't* have a leader. I said *one* leader is not enough anymore."

Blue's hand covered his, warm and reassuring. Blue's presence helped buoy his resolve, and he continued as his confidence in the new policy he wanted to implement, in the wisdom of it, returned. "Our pack is growing, but we can't continue living in the past or supporting an antiquated system that isn't fair for all our members. The only way to survive is to progress as a group."

The pack was still murmuring, talking quietly to one another, but their overall tone had lost its edge. He waited until he had their attention again. "Now, I'm not going to ask you to give up the traditions of this pack entirely. The stress would be too much to ask of anyone coming all at once. We

185

will still have an overall leader. What I'm suggesting is for us to also form a council. Each section of this society will elect a representative to a seat on this board. Not including the leader, it would mean we'd have a panel of four men or women who would represent the alphas, deltas, gammas, and omegas.

"The council will decide all matters of import to the pack, with the leader having the final vote. This way all interests will be represented, with no one group being shut out, just as no one group will have a distinct advantage over the rest." He cast a meaningful look at the alphas, the faction he knew would be most likely to disagree with his suggestion. Mac was fully ready to use his leader status to override them if they did, but it would be an easier transition for everyone if he could get the entire pack to agree to his plan.

"Think about it. It makes sense. Everyone gets a vote, and everyone's vote matters." Blue stood up next to him. "There's still a chain of command. You have a problem? You talk to your representative, and he or she brings it up at the council."

Mac nodded. "No more fights. No more violence. We'll need to hammer out the details yet -- for example, how long a leader will hold the staff and how long between elections."

The murmuring rose again, ebbing and swelling like the tide, threatening to swamp the meeting with only the smallest encouragement. Mac knew he had to regain control quickly before things got out of hand again. He noticed Elliot, an omega, raising his hand. "Elliot? You have a question?"

"We all have questions!" Cooper snarled at him.

Mac growled back. "And I'm doing my best to answer them!" He nodded toward Elliot. "What's your question, Elliot?"

Elliot looked around, his expression as nervous and wary

as a deer's, as if he were ready to bolt if anyone made any sudden moves. "H-how will the leader be chosen if not by challenge?"

"Good question. The answer is the same way the representatives will be chosen. We'll have an election. Anyone can run, male or female, alpha, delta, gamma, or omega, and whoever gets the most votes, wins."

Another alpha, one Mac didn't recognize, yelled out. "That's ridiculous! How do we know who's the strongest if there ain't no fight?"

Cooper agreed. "And how can a female lead? What if she catches pregnant while holding the leadership staff? A female is most vulnerable then. Everybody knows that."

"Women can lead just as well as men, Cooper!" Irvina Standish pushed her way to the front of the crowd. Two of Blue's youngest siblings clung to her skirt. "Maybe I'll run for leader. Couldn't do a worse job than you."

Argyle's eyes widened, and he struggled to his feet behind the table. "Irvina? You lost your ever-lovin' mind?"

"Good for you, Ma!" Blue waved at his mother. "Pa, let her be. It'd be her right to run, same as yours."

"Look, physical strength may have once determined if this pack would survive, but it's not as important anymore." Mac shook his head and gestured around the camp. "We don't need to fight for territory or to defend it against other packs. The human laws govern us, like it or not, but they also protect us. We own this land; the deed proving it is in the safe in the alpha cabin. I've seen it. Nobody can legally claim this mountain or trespass or hunt on our land without our approval." He glanced at Blue. "Which brings up another very important concern. We've found out something interesting. This mountain in rich in silver."

The crowd gasped as one. They mumbled the word "silver" and gaped at one another. They all knew how dangerous silver could be to them.

"That's right. Our mountain has a silver heart, and I don't need to tell you how unhealthy having silver so close is to all of us. I believe that's what's been fostering the violence and anger we've experienced for so long. Now, before anyone panics, I've figured out a way to get it out of our mountain." He took a deep breath and was grateful when he felt Blue's hand brush his in solidarity. "I've contracted with a mining company. They're going to come up the mountain and take the silver out. It won't be quick -- it's going to take several years, but when it's done, we'll be able to live here without fear of silver poisoning."

"Humans? You're going to let humans up here?" Cooper looked as stunned as everyone else.

"Yes. And while they're up here, we'll be living in a town called Hunter's Hollow. It's not far from here and still in the mountains, so it'll feel familiar to us. I bought the town -- signed the papers last week. There are houses enough for all of us. We'll order in enough provisions to see us comfortably through the winter, give us a head start on next year." He sighed. "I know this is a lot to take in. You'll need some time to process everything, and I promise to answer all your questions. But for now, that's how things stand."

"I don't know, Mac. A council of leaders? Okay, maybe, but women sitting on it? And moving? We've been here for tens of generations!" Argyle shook his head.

Blue crossed his arms over his chest and nodded. "Mac is right, Pa. Our survival depends on more than physical strength now. We have to be flexible. Our leaders need to be smart, to be cunning. We need people who can interact with the humans when necessary and solve our problems without resorting to violence. That could be a woman as well as a man."

"You mean somebody like you, Blue? Is that what you're saying?" Cooper sneered at him. "You don't have half the brain God gave a gopher. Don't think Mac is much smarter, neither, no matter what ten-dollar words he uses. Gonna uproot us all? Bring us to some town nobody never heard of? What bullshit is this?"

Blue growled at him. "You know, I'm getting really sick of your mouth, Cooper. Right now, this pack's leader is Mac, and you better start showing him some goddamn respect, or I might have to return to the old ways despite what he says and tear your fucking throat out."

"Fuck you, Blue. You think because you suck Mac's dick you can just—"

Blue howled, but Mac put out an arm, keeping Blue from jumping over the table and charging at Cooper.

"Settle down, Blue." He spoke louder, addressing the pack. "Everybody settle down!"

He might have kept Blue from attacking, but the pack was in an uproar again. People were shouting out questions along with hurling accusations.

"What's that mean? Was Enoch right about them?"

"I knew it! I knew those two were queer for each other!"

"Argyle! Did you know your boy was queer?"

"What if they turn the pups gay? What'll happen to us then?"

"I knew they couldn't be trusted, neither of them."

Mac took the leadership staff and banged it down on the porch. He kept it up until the crowd finally quieted again and reluctantly looked to him for answers. "Let's get one thing straight from the get-go -- it doesn't matter in the slightest who sleeps with who when it comes to being an effective leader. Your clan doesn't matter and neither does your sex or your sexuality. Next person who throws out an insult at me or Blue is apt to get this staff shoved up their asses. Got it?"

He glared at the crowd and was pleased to see most of the troublemakers, including Cooper, avert their gazes in submission. He knew he hadn't changed their minds -- only time would do that, if at all, although hopefully getting away from the silver would help -- but at least he'd given them something to think about. "Now, who I am doesn't matter anyway. I told you I didn't want to be leader, and I meant it. I plan to go back to the city, to my life. I'm only staying long enough to get the pack relocated to Hunter's Hollow, see the council up and running, and a new leader elected."

Blue's hand tugged hard on his arm, forcing Mac's body sideways. He found himself looking into Blue's stormy dark eyes. Blue looked absolutely furious. "What? What the hell do you mean, you're leaving?"

CHAPTER 20

Mac glanced at the crowd, realizing all eyes were on them. The last thing he wanted to give them were front-row seats to a private argument between himself and Blue, especially now, after he'd just managed to quash the homophobic rants that'd started to rise.

"Not now, Blue. We'll talk later, okay?"

"Fuck no. We'll talk right now. You've said what you needed to say to them. It's my turn." Blue growled at him, and Mac was impressed more than he wanted to be at Blue's alpha display. Something stirred deep in his belly in response. Blue was drop-dead sexy when he was pissed.

Mac kept his voice down, not wanting the pack to hear him capitulate so quickly to Blue's demand. "Okay, okay. Just give me a minute."

"You've got sixty seconds. Fifty-nine. Fifty-eight…"

He cleared his throat and turned back to the crowd. "Okay, folks. That's it for now. I think we all have enough to think about. Go on home, talk about what I said, consider whether you'd like to run for a council seat or even for leader or who you'd like to see in those roles. Start making plans to pack up your belongings. We'll meet again tomorrow after-noon to finish hashing things out."

He turned and followed Blue inside the cabin, suddenly feeling more apprehensive than he had when facing down the entire pack. Closing the door on the outside world came as a relief though. He hadn't realized how anxious he was feeling until immersed into the relative quiet of the cabin.

His newfound calm lasted only as long as it did for Blue to turn around and glare at him. The look on Blue's face made Mac's stomach feel like it was sinking into his shoes. "Blue, come on, now. I'm tired; you're tired. It's been a really long day, and the last thing either of us need is to fight."

"You fucker! You knew all along that you were leaving, but you never thought to clue me in?"

"I didn't think I had to! I have a life out there. I have a job. Friends. I didn't come out here to stay. I sure as shit never wanted to be leader. If you remember, I told you that first off."

Blue was visibly shaking. The muscles in his jaw jumped, and a vein throbbed in his neck. "Yeah? Well, the way you took right to it, I figured you changed your mind."

"Come on. I did what I had to do for the good of this pack."

"Why did you come back, Mac?"

Mac froze for a moment, unsure of how to answer. The truth seemed so petty, now that he knew what dire straits some of the pack members had been in. It was the truth, though, and he knew that no matter what, he didn't want to lie to Blue, not even if it made Mac look like a smug, selfish bastard.

"I came back to prove to everybody that I'm not useless, that I have worth. I was just a kid when they threw me away, Blue, and I wanted to show them how well I've done so they could be sorry I was banished. I wanted to rub my success in their faces."

"So, we're done then? You're going back to the city. It's over." Blue seemed to deflate, as if all the air had been let out of him. "It's my own damn fault. I let myself believe... Oh, never mind. It doesn't fucking matter." He turned away, shoulders slumped.

Mac frowned and placed a hand on Blue's shoulder. "Blue, wait. What we've got going together, it doesn't have to end. You can come back to the city with me."

"Me? In the city?" Blue shook his head. "I'm a mountain boy. All those buildings and people... I could never fit in there. I need to shift, to run. I don't know how you did it all those years."

"I did it because I didn't have a choice. I had to do it or die."

Blue turned back, his eyes brighter than they'd been a moment before. "That's just it, Mac! You don't have to do it anymore. You have a place here. You're leader. Even if you don't want to be anymore, if you want to give it up, you're still one of us. You still belong."

"So, you're saying...what? That I should throw away my career to stay? I just told you why I came back. It was to show off my wealth. Why would I leave it behind?"

Blue's lips hitched in a half smile. "Because when you had the opportunity to shove their faces in your success, you didn't do it. Instead, you used your money to help the pack. You paid to have Enoch put in a retirement home. You worked like a dog harvesting ginseng, and then when you sold it, you gave the money to the pack. You've always had the pack's best interest at heart, no matter how much you say otherwise."

Mac sighed. "Maybe, but I like photography, Blue. I miss it."

"Can't you take pictures up here? Or over at Hunter's Hollow? There's lots of interesting stuff to photograph in the mountains."

"That's true, but—"

"I don't want you to leave, Mac. Please don't go. The pack needs you, but more than that, *I* need you."

The bald candidness in Blue's expression shook Mac to his core. No one had ever wanted him to stick around so badly that they'd begged for him to stay. No one had ever cared about him enough. Not the pack when he'd been thrown out, not his associates in the human world when he told them he was going home.

Only Blue wanted him. Only Blue begged him not to go.

"I have to think about it, Blue. It's a big step, giving up everything I worked so hard to get."

"That's as much as I can hope for, isn't it? A maybe?" Blue sighed and knelt down in front of the fireplace. He gathered kindling in preparation for starting a fire. Mac suspected it had more to do with having something to do, something to distract Blue from the strong emotions he must be feeling, than for any need for warmth.

Mac squatted on his haunches and grabbed both of Blue's hands. "I didn't say no. I just said I have to think about." He bit his lip, then grinned. "Come on, Blue. Let's shift and go for a good run. I haven't shifted since I fought Luc."

"Speaking of, what are you going to do about him? Or are you going to leave the problem of Luc for the next leader?"

"I guess I deserve that."

Blue shook his head. "No, you don't. I'm just lashing out." His cheek hitched in a small smile, and he wiped at his eyes with his sleeve. "Okay. Let's run. I could use the exercise. Is the pack still out there?"

Mac grinned and stood up, then reached down to offer

Blue a hand. He looked out the window. "I think they've all gone home. The coast looks clear."

"Good. Let's go. We can head up to the cabin by the logging camp and leave our clothes there. Then we can shift and run on the mountain. No one will be around up there to bother us."

* * *

LETTING his wolf-self run free had never felt so liberating to Mac. In the city, shifting was always done covertly, with trepidation and fraught with the fear of being discovered. The couple of times he'd shifted on the mountain since his return had been to fight. He'd never shifted for the simple joy of being his wolf-self, to run free, He felt the crunch of leaves under his paws and scented the wind, letting the air tell him everything he needed to know.

There was a rabbit warren near the roots of that old oak. A fox had run this way a few hours before. There was a black bear that enjoyed using this hickory tree for a scratching post. A small group of deer followed this trail down to Jewel Creek, three does and two fawn. A buck followed behind them. Big one, maybe an eight-pointer.

He burst through the brush into a small meadow. The grass grew taller than his head, slender stalks rippling in the breeze. He and Blue jumped through it like a pair of pups out for their first run. They played tag, one nipping at the other's haunches then racing away, the other following suit a moment or two later. Running in wide circles, yipping like children, he felt pure joy course through his veins.

Blue finally flopped down on the ground, panting, and Mac joined him. His sides heaved, and it took several moments for him to catch his breath again. He couldn't remember the last time he'd run just for the fun of it. Before he was banished, for sure. He lay on his stomach and rested his shaggy head on his front paws, letting the sun warm his back.

I'm glad you asked me to run, Blue. I'd almost forgotten how wonderful it is.

God, you smell good. You smell like the mountain, Mac. Blue nosed Mac's head, sniffing. *Didn't you run in the city?*

Mac turned his head and gave Blue's muzzle a lick. *Yeah, I ran, but not like this. I always had to be so careful not to get caught. They have dogcatchers in the city, humans who would've taken me to a shelter. I also had to watch out for cars, and dogs.*

What's a shelter?

It's a place where the humans take stray dogs and cats. If no one claims them, they get put down.

Blue's head popped up, and he snapped at the air. *You mean they* kill *us? And we* let *them? Why? What gives humans the right to murder us? Why don't the shifters just tear their fucking throats out?*

Mac whined a little, trying to reassure Blue. *Most of the ones they catch aren't shifters, Blue. They're dogs and cats—they can't fight back.*

Poor things. Humans are fucking brutal, Mac.

Yeah, they can be. Not all of them, though. One of the charities I support is a no-kill shelter. With enough funding, they take care of the animals no one wants.

Their thoughts fell silent, and eventually Mac drifted off to sleep. He woke to Blue nudging him in the side.

Hey, sleepyhead. Time to get up. I'm hungry, and it's getting cold.

To Mac's surprise, he didn't want to go home. It was so peaceful, being up on the mountain with Blue, happy and stress-free. He didn't want to go back to where the problems waited for him, both the pack's issues and his own decision whether or not to leave.

If he went back to the city, he'd have his photography career. He'd also go back to shifting only when absolutely necessary and always with apprehension, always staying in the shadows, nothing but hard concrete or asphalt beneath his paws, the stench of the city strong in his nose.

If he stayed, he'd have Blue and lazy afternoons spent running free on the mountain, breathing fresh, clean air, and feeling soft grass under his feet. Plus, he could put a studio in Blue's cabin. He could take all the photographs he wanted and use a satellite hookup to email them to his agent.

It was, after all, the digital age.

He wondered why he'd ever been stressed about leaving the pack in the first place. It didn't seem like he had to make such a difficult choice after all. In fact, the answer seemed obvious.

Blue was right. He was already where he belonged.

He was home.

Yipping like a pup, he jumped into the air for the sheer joy of it, twisting his body as he came down and tackling Blue to the ground. They play-wrestled like kids, then ran down the mountain toward the cabin.

Mac was first through the open door and shifted back into his man-form as soon as he cleared the threshold. He turned around just in time for Blue to hit him full force in the chest, knocking him to the ground. A wet, warm tongue licked his face as a warm, shaggy body wriggled against him in excitement.

Then, where there was once fur, there was soft skin and hard muscle instead. The tongue licking him was still warm and wet, but it was human now and pushing into his mouth with a hunger he returned in force.

"Tell me you'll stay." Blue's voice was soft and sexy, lips moving, kissing his way over Mac's jaw to his throat.

Mac arched his neck to give Blue better access to the delicate skin under his jaw. "Yes. Yes, damn it, I'll stay! Fuck, Blue, how could I ever have considered leaving? This is where I belong. And you're the one I belong *to.*"

"Fucking A." Blue's dick rubbed against Mac's thigh, hard and hot and an impressive indication of Blue's desire for him. "Mine."

"Yours."

Mac lay back, enjoying the feel of Blue's mouth working its way down his chest to his groin. When Blue took his length in, he moaned with pure pleasure. He threaded his fingers into Blue's hair and gave himself over fully to Blue's attentions.

Home.

Love.

Mate.

Yours, he thought. *And you're mine. Forever.*

CHAPTER 21

"How's he doing, Ma?"

Mac had gone to his parents' cabin to visit and to share the news that he'd decided to stay with the pack. He also wanted to check on Luc's progress. The sooner Luc regained his health, the sooner Mac would need to decide what to do. Blue had been right about one thing-- it wasn't fair to leave the problem of Luc to the next leader. This was Mac's mess, and he needed to finish cleaning it up.

As it turned out, it wasn't too difficult a problem to surmount after all.

"Not too good, Mac. I mean physically, he's getting on fine. His bones is healing, and he ain't got no more fever." Sylva poured boiling water into a pair of mugs, then carried them over to the table, offering one to Mac. She glanced toward the pallet at the back of the cabin where Luc lay and lowered her voice to a whisper, although wolf ears would hear it just as well as if she'd screamed it. "But his mind is gone."

"What do you mean?" Mac helped himself to honey, pouring a healthy dollop into his tea, then stirring it before taking a sip. Chamomile. He should've known. His ma always knew when he needed to relax.

"Exactly what I say, son. Luc's mind ain't what it was. Maybe it was the fight or maybe the fever that set in after done it, but he's like a child now. He likes to play dolls with Amie, and Lord help me if he don't suck his thumb."

Mac frowned, looking toward the back corner. Luc lay on his side, stretched out on a pallet, playing with Amie and a couple of other children. When he laughed, it was with the abandon of a child.

Mac lowered his voice to a whisper. "Think he could be faking it, Ma?"

She shook her head. "No. I see him twenty-four hours a day, seven days a week, Mac. If he was faking, I'd know."

"Well, now what do I do? I can't banish him. It would be a death sentence for sure. If he's not right in the head, he'd never survive alone. But I'm afraid nobody in the pack will want him either."

"Your pa and I talked it over. We'll take him in."

Mac's eyes flashed open wide. "What? Why would you do that?"

"Because wolves should take care of their own. Yes, he caused a lot of trouble. He hurt my boy. But I think he's paying the price now." She glanced over at Luc again. "And he's good with the children. A help, really. He watches out for the little ones."

"Are you sure?"

She nodded. "Yes. It's the right thing to do. A healer can't just toss a sick man out when there ain't nobody else to care for him."

"You're a good woman, Ma. And Pa is a good man."

She harrumphed and sipped her tea, then looked at him over the rim of her cup. "So, you staying, or are you going back to the human world?"

He grinned at her. "You already know my answer, don't you?"

She smiled back at him. "I knew you were home to stay from the moment I walked out on the porch of this cabin and saw you'd come back. A mother knows, Mac."

"I'm going to be with Blue." He looked down at the cup in his hand, feeling his cheeks heat up. He hadn't meant to say it so bluntly.

"I figured as much. You love him."

"Yes, ma'am. I do."

"And I reckon he loves you back?"

"So he says. He's my mate, Ma, and I'm his."

She nodded and put her cup down. "Then you go and be happy, son. In the end, that's all that matters. 'Course, I'd be lying if I said I wouldn't like to see the grandchildren you'd have brung me, but we can't have everything, huh?"

"No, ma'am, we can't." He smiled and stood up, then went to get a hug from her. "Thank you, Ma. Where's Pa? I'm afraid he's not going to take the news as well as you did."

"Oh, now you leave him to me and don't worry. Go on, now. You got work to do, don't you? I think you have a meeting you need to run."

"Shoot! I didn't realize how late it was getting." He nodded and kissed her cheek. "Thanks again, Ma. You're the best."

"Aw, go on with you." She fluttered her hands, waving him away. "And tell that alpha mate of yours I expect you both for Sunday supper."

* * *

THE PACK'S very first election came soon after they were safely ensconced in Hunter's Hollow. The move had actually gone relatively smoothly and with far less trouble than Mac anticipated. He felt it was anticlimactic after all the trouble he'd had convincing everyone they had to move in the first place.

Hunter's Hollow was a nice little town -- or it would be once the pack finished fixing it up. There were several dozen houses, most in relatively good repair, and a full street of storefronts, including an abandoned hair salon, to the delight of most of the ladies and several of the men.

Mac had also seen that a playground was installed for the pups to play on, and there were delighted shrieks of laughter floating across Main Street all day. There was also a small school, which the pack teachers immediately claimed.

Once they were settled, Mac set a date for the election. Mac also ordered each candidate who declared for leader, as well as the people who wanted the posts of representatives, to give a speech to the pack.

In the end, it was a delta female who finally took the leadership staff.

Her name was Emma Story. She was an older woman with steel gray threading through her dark hair, and kindly, yet sharp eyes that seemed to miss nothing. When she walked, her back was ramrod straight, and she spoke with both passion and fierceness.

When Emma stepped up on the porch and spoke, her voice, although softer than some of the more blustery male candidates, especially the alphas, drew the attention of the crowd, and her words resonated with almost everyone there.

"I've lived all my life serving this pack. You all know me. We've worked together and played together. I've cried with you during the bad times and laughed with you during the good times. Our wolf-selves have run together under the same moon. I know you because I *am* you.

"There's nothing I want more than to help this pack

become stronger, smarter, and safer because you're my family. And to me, nothing is more important than that."

The ballots were cast in secret, each person writing the name of their choice on a piece of paper and depositing it into a large wooden box. Blue pulled each piece of paper out and read the name on it, and Mac kept the tally.

When Mac announced the winner, there was some huffing and puffing from the alphas, but in the end, they accepted Emma as the pack's choice for leader.

Mac handed her the staff, and as he did, he felt as if a great load was lifted from his shoulders. He didn't really understand the amount of stress he'd been under until he was finally freed of it.

The change in leadership was marked by a celebration, a party held in the common area in front of the alpha cabins. Everyone brought food, which was set out buffet-style. Someone got out a fiddle, and music filled the air.

Mac found himself dancing with several women, each one taking his arm and trying to steal him away from the others. He smiled good-naturedly and clomped around, trying to keep time to the music and not step on anyone's toes. Dancing was definitely *not* in his wheelhouse.

Finally, he begged off and went in search of Blue. He spotted Blue do-si-do-ing with two of Blue's younger sisters, and was on his way over to them when Emma stopped him.

"Mac, I'd like to talk to you and Blue if you have a minute."

"Sure thing, Madam Alpha." He smiled and gave her a little bow.

"Hmph. Best make it Madam Leader. I was born a delta, and I'll die one." Emma grinned and crossed her arms over her chest. "'Sides, Madam Leader sounds regal-like."

Mac chuckled. "Let me grab Blue. We'll meet you over at the alpha cabin, okay?"

She nodded and headed in that direction.

Mac stepped up to Blue, who was in the middle of a promenade with one of his sisters. "Blue? Emma wants to talk to us."

"Oh? Okay. Sorry, Sissy. Gotta go do grown-up stuff now."

"Aw, Blue! You promised!" The girl was no more than eight or nine years old, and her lip jutted out in a proper pout.

"I'll dance with you later. Promise."

"Yeah, you'd better or I'm telling Ma!"

Blue stuck his tongue out at her, and she replied with a loud raspberry.

Mac chuckled and led Blue away. "You better keep your word to her, Blue. She sounds like she means business."

"She does. She'd squeal on me in two shakes. So, what does Emma want us for?"

There was nothing Mac could do but shrug. He had no idea either. "Guess we'll find out soon enough."

Mac rapped on the alpha cabin's door, then opened it and ushered Blue inside. Emma was seated at the table with her husband and children. The four elected representatives, three men and one woman, were seated around a cheerfully crackling fire. Everyone looked up as Mac and Blue entered the cabin.

"I need a moment to speak with Mac and Blue and the representatives, dear. Would you take the children outside?" Emma smiled at her mate. He nodded and gathered up the children, carrying the youngest, and herded the rest of them out the door. She waited until the door closed before speaking again. "Thank you for coming, Mac, Blue."

Blue gave her a short bow. "No problem, Madam Alpha."

Mac elbowed him. "She prefers 'Madam Leader.'"

She chuckled and held up a hand. "Please, I've known you

since you were in diapers, Blue Standish! We don't need to be so formal. Emma will do just fine."

Blue smiled at her. "Okay, Emma. What can we do for you?"

"I want to know about ginseng."

Mac and Blue exchanged a knowing look. "Oh?"

She nodded, but the smile left her face. "Blue, your family has been logging on the mountain for generations."

A tiny frown creased the skin between Blue's eyebrows. "Yup. Almost since we first settled in the valley."

"That may be a problem." Emma reached for a laptop computer, a new addition since they'd moved to Hunter's Hollow and a promising clue to the evolution of the pack, and turned the screen so Mac and Blue could read it. "I've been reading these reports on deforestation. I think our mountain has taken about all the logging it can handle. There are bald patches on it where it will take generations for the new growth to mature."

Blue nodded. "I know. We've talked about it as a clan, but what can we do? Timber is the only source of income for the pack, aside from what the Fullers bring in with their moonshine."

Emma's mouth set in a hard line. "You might as well know, Mac, I'll be talking to your pa about the 'shine business later. I worry about taking the risk of making illegal 'shine and selling it to humans. It's too dangerous for the pack." She shook her head and waved a hand as if dismissing the thought. "That's a problem for later, but timber is why I wanted to talk to you now. The logging has to stop, but we need something to replace the income. I think ginseng might be the answer."

Mac grinned. "I think you may be right, Emma. We earned a lot of money last ginseng season, and it was only Blue and me who harvested. This area is similar to our mountain. It must grow here too. Plus, we can raise it. It takes a few years for a ginseng farm to produce and turn a profit though. In the meantime, working together, the pack could earn enough to sustain itself all year on what we harvest during the three months of ginseng season."

Emma nodded. "But we have to do it right. You said something the day you announced the elections, Mac, that stuck with me. You said human laws governed us but also protected us."

"Yes, I remember."

"There are human laws governing ginseng, right?"

"I believe so. I think there are permits you need to get to collect it legally, even on your own land."

Emma gave a sharp nod, as if her decision was made. "Then that's what we'll need to do. I don't want any trouble from the humans, so if we need to get a permit, then we will. I want you to help with that, if you don't mind. Will you be our go-between with the humans?"

Mac cocked his head, then exchanged a look with Blue. "Like a liaison?"

Emma laughed. "Is that what it's called? You know I'm just a simple country girl, Mac. I don't know a lot of ten-dollar words."

Blue snorted. "I think you know a lot more than you let on, Emma. You're smarter than a lot of folks around here."

She blushed. "Well, be that as it may, will you? I'll need you to go see about getting us those permits when the time comes. I'll also need you to teach the pack how to find ginseng, how to collect it, and how to store it. And we'll need your help when it comes to selling it, as well, and starting the farm."

"We'd be happy to help with whatever we can," Mac said.

Blue nodded in agreement. "Absolutely. And I'll tell my pa about the logging. The Standishes might not be too happy about it, but I know they'll do what's right for the pack. Now, if you don't mind, I have a favor to ask you."

Emma blinked, then smiled. "Of course. What is it?"

"Mac and I would like to build a new cabin on the outskirts of town. There's a little creek we found that reminds us of Jewel Creek. Traditionally, the leader needs to give permission for any new construction."

Emma's smile grew wide. "Is that all? Of course! You've done so much for the pack; you deserve to build whatever you want, wherever you want."

"Thanks, Emma." Mac grabbed Blue's hand and squeezed it. "We're going to get started right away. We'd like it to be done before the first snowfall."

Emma shook her head and looked sad. "I'm sorry, but I don't think that's going to happen."

Mac blinked. "Why not? You just said we could build wherever we wanted."

She pointed to the window. "Because I'm afraid you're too late. It's already started snowing."

They turned and looked. Outside, fat white flakes were drifting down from the sky in lazy spirals. Patches of white dotted the ground.

Blue nudged Mac with a shoulder. "Guess we'll have to hunker down in the house we claimed until the spring thaw."

Mac grinned and felt his cheeks heating up. Truth be told, there was nothing he'd like better than to get snowed in with Blue for the cold season in a cozy cabin with a warm fire and a soft bed.

EPILOGUE

Mac got his wish. The snow that started while they were in the cabin talking to Emma never let up. It got heavier and thicker and fell faster until it became the first full-blown blizzard of the season. By the next morning, there was two feet of fresh snow on the ground. Mac was very glad he'd thought to lay in provisions to see the pack through the winter before they moved.

The storms blew in with regularity, but gradually the winds grew milder, and winter finally melted into spring. When warmer winds blew, the first greens appeared. It seemed the mountains woke up again overnight, covered in colorful wildflowers and fresh greenery.

Blue and Mac built their cabin close enough to Little Creek -- the name they gave the meandering stream they'd found -- for convenience, but far enough away that flooding wasn't an issue. The cabin was fairly large, having four rooms on the first floor and a full loft that Mac outfitted for his studio.

Mac couldn't remember being happier. He had Blue, of course, and he had his family close by. The pack was growing fat and content, led by a powerful woman who actually had the pack's best interest at heart. The representatives were working well too. They helped soothe irritations before things escalated and brought new ideas to Emma for consideration.

One afternoon, he and Blue went to visit Sylva and Angus. No one was home except for the children and Luc.

"Hey, Mac. Hey, Blue. Come to play with us?" Luc looked up from where he was playing jacks with Aimee, and gave them a big smile.

"Maybe later, Luc. Where's Ma and Pa?"

Aimee jumped up for a hug from each of them. "Pa's taking his turn cutting firewood, and Ma's out at the Clarke cabin. Mary Jo is having her baby. She's been gone a while though."

Just then the door opened, and Sylva walked inside. She had a small bundle in her arms, wrapped up in a faded quilt. "Blue! Mac! Just the two people I wanted to see."

"Hey, Ma!" Mac stepped up to kiss his mother on the cheek when he noticed the bundle she carried move. "What's that?"

"Not what. Who." She smiled as she peeled back a corner of the quilt, exposing a sweet little face. "Her name is April— for the month."

"Is this Mary Jo Clarke's baby? Why do you have her?"

Sylva sighed. "Mary Jo has six other children, and her husband passed on three months ago. You remember? Heart attack. So young too." She shook her head sadly. "She's still in mourning, and certainly isn't ready to mate again, but she can barely take care of the children she already has. I saw the pain it caused her, but she did what was best for the child. She asked me if I knew of anyone who would take her baby, who'd love it and take care of it. I said I did."

KIERNAN KELLY

Blue walked up to them and stroked the baby's cheek with one finger. "You did? Who?"

Sylva smiled at them and looked up at Mac. "You two."

Mac gasped. "Us? Parents? What made you think that we'd... I mean, a baby?"

"A baby." Blue's voice was soft, and his gaze was warm. "A baby, Mac. Our daughter."

Mac looked down and touched the baby's tiny hand. April's miniscule hand wrapped around his finger, holding tight as if she didn't want to let go. In that moment, his heart was lost. He looked at Blue and nodded. "Our daughter."

Sylva handed the baby to Blue, who cradled her carefully in his arms. Mac slipped an arm around Blue and held his new family close.

"Hello, April." Blue's smile looked soft and heartbreakingly beautiful to Mac. "Welcome home."

A fire lit inside Mac's soul, and it burned so brightly and so fiercely it brought tears to his eyes. He was amazed at how much in his life had changed and how far he'd come. Just last year, he'd been without a single soul who cared about him. No pack, no family, no one to love, no one who cared if he lived or died except for those who bought his photographs.

Now he had everything he'd ever hoped for and so much more. He had a mate who he adored and who loved him back, a pack that'd learned to respect him, and now a daughter he already knew he'd die to protect.

His life hadn't been easy. He'd been born on the wrong side of the tracks, and there'd been times when he wasn't sure he would survive, but now he knew without a doubt he wouldn't change a thing even if he could. The road had been harsh, but it'd led him to Something he'd never even known he'd wanted -- a family of his own.

He was finally and truly home.

www.ingramcontent.com/pod-product-compliance
Lightning Source LLC
Chambersburg PA
CBHW060926180626
46817CB00004B/1412